Ivy & Mistletoe

Also By Nicole Mullaney

Magic in Mount Holly (coming soon)
The Maltese Holiday (coming soon)
Deck the Heart (coming soon)

Also check out books written by character Ethan Dulane

Joy and Hope

For Adult Romance Check out Nikki A Lamers

<u>The Unforgettable Series:</u>
The Unforgettable Summer
Unforgettable Nights
Unforgettable Dreams
Unforgettable Memories
The Unforgettable One

<u>The Home Duet:</u>
Dreams Lost and Found
Finding Home

By Nicole Mullaney

Based on the Screenplay by Candy Cain

Table of Contents

Copyright

Frey Dreams an imprint of Nikki A Lamers

ISBN 978-1-95-1185-12-1 (paperback)
ISBN 978-1-95-1185-03-9 (ebook)

Image by Lauren Halla Celi, owner and photographer of "A Moment in Time Photography"

Cover design by Constantine Chutis

Dedication

This book is dedicated to my dad, William T. Frey. Some of my fondest memories with you include a book, a movie or both. I miss you every single day, Dad! I love you lots and lots!

Chapter 1

Ivy

"I can't believe my flight is cancelled," I grumble to myself. I want to be home for Christmas, not spending it here alone. I heave a sigh and grimace at my reflection in the mirror of the airport bathroom, trying to figure out my next move. I'm a mess and I haven't even left Charleston yet. My pale blue eyes appear slightly defeated and my light blonde hair already has loose strands falling out of the French braid I put it in this morning. I lightly brush a lock of hair behind my ear and push my braid back over my shoulder. I force myself to smile, but even that doesn't make me feel any better. I pull my indigo blue cable knit sweater down over my dark gray jeans, thankful I at least thought to dress comfortable today. I grip the handle of my large, black suitcase and grumble, "Well, I can't sit in the airport all day, waiting for a miracle. I have to figure out what to do." I tip my suitcase up and roll it behind me as I stride out of the bathroom and towards the exit.

I walk out of Charleston airport and back into sixty-degree warmth and sunshine with a groan of frustration. I trudge towards the parking lot, attempting to remind myself how lucky I am. I really shouldn't complain, but with Christmas only a few days away, I can't help it. I want to be with my family, watching the snowfall outside the window at my parent's house in Boston. I want to bake Christmas cookies with my family. I want to open presents with my twin brother, Sawyer. I want to see Christmas trees decorated with lights and real snow, not palm trees with Christmas lights and cotton because even though cotton is white, it doesn't look anything like snow. Unfortunately, the northeast has a major snowstorm heading directly for it, grounding all flights flying into or out of the area on the same day I'm supposed to be flying home. Now I have to scramble to figure out a different way to get home to Boston.

I pause to pull my cell phone out of my purse, dreading the phone call I have to make to my mom right now, but it's better to get it over with. She's not going to be happy. I guess it will be easier to call her than my dad. Dad will try to control the situation, since he always tries to fix everything. Besides, it's not like he can do anything from there anyway, unless he's a good friend of Mother Nature. I glance at the time and grimace. I have to let them know what's going on, before they leave for the airport to pick me up. I take a deep breath in anticipation as I tap my mom's name. I wait for her to pick up before I continue walking towards my car, dragging my suitcase behind me. "Hi, Ivy," my mom's soft voice comes through the line. I can't help, but picture her tucking her straight, shoulder length brown hair behind her ear, like that will help her hear me better.

"Hi, Mom," I reply, not able to hide my displeasure from my voice.

"Ivy, Sweetheart, where are you? Are you at the airport? Is your flight going to leave on time?" my mom asks, anxiously.

I grimace and complain, "No! I'm still at the airport, but as of right now, I can't get a flight out until the day after Christmas, Mom. Everything is cancelled." I finally reach my car, an old light blue Mazda 3 and stop behind it. I quickly open the trunk and reach for my suitcase. I lift it up off the ground and set it down inside the trunk, putting it back in the same spot I took it out of less than an hour ago.

My mom attempts to make me feel better, but I hear the disappointment in her delayed reaction all the same. "Don't worry, sweetie. Everything happens for a reason. We'll just postpone Christmas until you get here," she proposes in an attempt to comfort me.

I gasp and slam the trunk of my car closed, shocked by her suggestion. "Postpone Christmas? No way!" I proclaim. I quickly stride for the driver's side door as an idea suddenly pops into my head. I make a quick decision, wondering why I didn't think of it sooner. "I'm just going to drive," I announce. I'm determined to make it home for the holidays. A little bit of snow isn't going to stop me. I pull the door open and slip my petite frame behind the wheel, before pulling the door shut behind me.

"What?" mom questions, sounding completely stunned. "You can't drive, Ivy!" she declares. "That's twenty hours driving all by yourself." She pauses and then emphasizes, "Charleston to Boston is a twenty hour drive."

I click my seat belt into place and inform her, with confidence, "Sixteen, and that's with stopping. I can beat the storm, Mom," I insist, hoping I'm right. I have to be. I hear her gasp again and I imagine the panic in her brown eyes. I quickly continue stopping her from saying anything else. "I'll see you tomorrow. Love you!" I exclaim. I disconnect the call before my mom can argue with me anymore, or bring my dad into the conversation. If that happened, I would've never gotten off the phone and then I definitely wouldn't make it home.

I start the car and back out of my parking spot. I pull out of the airport parking lot and drive away, but instead of turning back towards my apartment here in Charleston, I veer my car towards Boston, happy with my decision. I have a lot to think about anyway. Driving home by myself will give me a lot more time to do that, but I'm going to make it home.

Moments later my phone rings. I glance at the screen and see "Dad," flash across my screen. I laugh to myself and mumble, "Of course." I ignore it, letting it go to voicemail while I'm driving. At the next red light, I reach for my phone and tap messages. I put my phone on speaker and then tap play. I drop my phone into the cup holder and wait to hear my Dad's deep voice, echoing throughout my small car.

"Ivy, it's Dad," he declares. I grin at his authoritative tone. My dad is a big guy, but he has the softest heart in the world. "Don't drive home," he demands. "You're going to get stuck. This storm is going to be a doozy. Do you understand me, Ivy Louise Anderson?" he questions, warning me. I try not to roll my eyes at the use of my middle name. Sometimes I wonder if they remember I'm an adult and I can make my own decisions. "Do not drive!" he emphasizes again. I giggle to myself and shake my head, knowing he would be doing the exact same thing as me, right now, if he were in my shoes. We've never spent Christmas apart and I don't want that to start now, or ever. Then again, Mom does always say I get my stubborn side from my Dad.

I'm one of the few people I know that doesn't have a streaming service or some kind of satellite radio. A road trip like this is the only time I feel like I really need one. I flip on the radio, tuning to my favorite local station, as the last few notes of a Christmas song echo around me. I merge onto the highway as a melodic, but powerful female voice comes through my car speakers. "You're listening to 'Live it Up' with Donna Drake. Be thankful that you're living in the south. The storm of the century is making its way through the Midwest to the northeast, dumping over six feet of snow in parts of the country."

My eyes widen in shock. Six feet is a lot of snow, but that has to be up in Maine or something. I wonder how much they're predicting Boston will get. I take a deep breath and exhale slowly, hoping the storm doesn't dump too much snow between here and Boston, at least not until after I make it home to my family.

"Bundle up and be glad you aren't dealing with such a bad blizzard. Airports in the northeast have been closed and hundreds of flights have been cancelled," she announces.

I grimace and mumble to myself, "You're not telling me anything new."

"Stay warm, Charleston. Here's 'Bring on the Snow' by Rorie Kelly." Soft, upbeat strums of an acoustic guitar flow through the speakers, just before a woman begins to sing about wanting snow. I chuckle at the irony as I drive north on the highway, trying to beat a snowstorm, while listening to a woman play her guitar and sing about a lot of snow.

I watch the green trees pass me by as I drive north, determined to make it home. I really need some time with my family to decompress and try to figure out what I'm going to do now that I'm out of a job. My boss said she'd give me an excellent recommendation and there's a few places in the same area looking for a new sous chef. There's even one that's hiring a new executive chef, but I'm not sure if I'm ready for that yet. Besides, I'm not even sure if I should stay in Charleston. I really enjoyed living there during school, but it's hard being so far away from my family sometimes, especially now that so many of my friends have moved on, finding jobs in all different locations. While I contemplate my future, palm trees become less and less, while pine trees become more and more. I leave South Carolina, drive through North Carolina, and then by the time I drive over the border into

Virginia, I don't see a palm tree in sight. My stomach growls, loudly, startling me out of my thoughts. I laugh at my reaction. I almost immediately notice a blue sign indicating a rest stop. I quickly merge to the right and pull off at the exit.

I park my car and walk inside the glass doors. Like many rest stops, this one has an open area, covered in dark brown tile floors, with square and rectangular tables and chairs spread throughout the middle. The convenience store and quick-service food restaurants are set up along the outside, in a sort of half circle. I use the restroom and wash my hands, before I grab myself something to eat along with some more coffee, to help keep me awake on the road. Only a few minutes later, I'm walking out with a brown paper bag in one hand and a cup of coffee in the other, in a hurry to get back on the road before it's too late.

My phone rings and I quickly switch the bag to the same hand as my coffee to pull my phone out of my pocket with a free hand. I smile upon seeing my twin brother, Sawyer's face on my screen. He's a little taller than me and his blonde hair is slightly darker than mine, but we both have the same blue eyes. He teased me a lot when we were younger, but even when we fight; he's always my best friend. I press answer and put my phone to my ear as I continue walking to my car. "Hi, Sawyer," I greet him with a wide smile on my face, even though he can't see me.

"Ivy," he utters my name with obvious relief. "I'm so glad you answered. Does that mean you're not driving here?" he prompts.

I grimace, not wanting to answer that question, but I know I have to. "No, I'm on my way. I just stopped at a rest stop in Virginia, I think, for a coffee and something to eat," I inform him, as I look around for a sign that might tell me exactly where I am.

"Oh, boy," he grumbles.

"It hasn't even started snowing yet," I tell him.

Sawyer heaves a sigh, "It's really bad here, Ivy. It started an hour ago. There's no way you're going to make it," he declares.

"Never say never," I announce, still determined, even with his weather update. "I'll be home by midnight," I maintain, just as I reach my car.

Sawyer sighs in defeat, knowing he's not about to change my mind. "Promise me that you'll stop if it gets too bad. Or if you get too tired," he emphasizes.

"Sawyer, you sound like mom. Relax. I'll be fine," I insist. "I'll see you soon," I proclaim and disconnect the call before he can argue with me anymore. I place my phone, coffee and the paper bag on the roof of the car as I search for my keys and open the car door.

I reach for my things on top of my car, just as a woman, dressed in a cobalt blue dress and a winter coat approaches, interrupting me. She's about the same height as me, with dark hair, rosy cheeks and bright, friendly eyes. "Excuse me?" she prods to get my attention.

I turn towards the woman and question, "Yes?"

"Do you know how far it is to Richmond?" she inquires, sounding hopeful.

I shake my head and offer her an apologetic smile. "No, I'm sorry. I don't. I'm not from around here," I explain.

She nods in acceptance and smiles in return. "Okay. Thanks, anyway. Merry Christmas!" she exclaims.

I return her contagious smile and offer her the same cheerful greeting, "Merry Christmas!"

The woman turns and strides towards the brick building. I look away from her and quickly grab my coffee and the brown paper bag from the roof of my car, before I slide in behind the wheel. I pull the door closed and swiftly start the car. I pull out of my parking spot and away from the rest stop, anxious to get back on the road and cover as much ground as I can before I have to stop for gas. I have to make my stops fast if I want to have a chance of beating this storm.

Almost immediately after I pull back onto the road, snow begins to fall, and the sun starts to set. I sigh and attempt to focus on the road in front of me. I try to relax, as I continue the drive. It's not too long before it's completely dark outside and the snow is falling hard and fast. The flakes begin sticking together and appear bigger and bigger, making it harder and harder to see the road. I heave another sigh and force myself to slow down, while I try to calculate how much further I have to go before I make it home.

I squint through the darkness and the falling snow, the road barely visible as I creep along. I sigh and reach over to the console for my phone. Then I lean further over to the passenger seat, trying to keep my eyes on the road. My hand touches something and I lift up the brown paper bag from the rest stop, now crumpled and filled with trash. My heart begins to pound harder and faster as I feel my anxiety creeping up on me. A flash of me putting my phone on top of my car causes my stomach to churn. "Oh, no. No, no, no, no, no!" I whine, hoping I'm wrong. I don't see anywhere to pull over with the snow beginning to pile up on the side of the road. So, I keep driving as I frantically attempt to search my car. I pull down the visor, then reach over and flip through the glove box, before I move back and search the center console one more time, to no avail. "No," I complain, again.

Having one last place to look, I try to keep my eyes on the road as I lean over and reach under the passenger seat, thinking it may have slipped underneath. My eyes briefly lose sight of the road. Seconds later, a loud horn blast startles me straight back into my seat. I gasp and tightly clench the wheel with both hands. I attempt to veer away from the on-coming vehicle. I swerve, pulling the wheel hard to the right. I inhale quickly and hold my breath as I feel the wheels slip on the snow and ice. The other car passes by me safely, as I try to correct the direction my car is moving. I stop suddenly, my breath whooshing from my lungs, as my seatbelt locks into place and snow appears to fly all around me in a wall of white. I clench the steering wheel tightly, turning my knuckles white. I stare straight ahead with wide eyes and my mouth dropped open in shock. I give myself a mental shake, attempting to pull myself out of the stupor. Then, I put my car in park and drop my head to the steering wheel as I breathe a sigh of relief.

I take a few more deep breaths to calm myself down and make sure I'm okay, before I lift my head and look around me. I grimace, realizing I slid off the side of the road into a ditch filled with snow. I put my car in reverse and try to back out, but my wheels don't do anything, but spin. I put my car into drive, hoping I can go forward instead, continuing into a wide turn. I push on the gas, but all I hear is the low rumble of my engine and the high pitch of my spinning tires on the snow. I throw the car into park and groan in frustration, "Ugh! Why? Why? Why?" I yell, banging on the steering wheel for emphasis. "This is not fair! Come on! I just want to get home for Christmas!" I whine.

I hit the steering wheel one last time, giving in. I unbuckle my seat belt with a defeated sigh. I reach for my black, gray and red plaid dress coat and slip it on. I wrap my red scarf around my neck and pull on my black gloves. I glance both ways into the dark before I push my door open and step out of the car into the snow. I suppress a shiver and look both ways again, hoping for any sign of a car or truck on the road. I groan in annoyance when I don't hear anything but the wind, blowing the falling snow. I take a couple steps towards the back of my car to see what's behind me, but I don't notice anything except snow. Then I walk towards the front of the car and my eyes widen at the sight of a flat tire. I heave a sigh, suddenly feeling completely alone and beaten. I slide back into my car and pull the door shut behind me, shivering.

"What am I going to do?" I ask myself, anxiously. I flip on my hazard lights and drop my head against my window, resting it there. I close my eyes, frustrated with myself and completely exhausted. I feel myself starting to fall asleep, as I pray someone will find me quickly.

Chapter 2

Max

"My phone is about to die Lucy and I left my charger at home. Unfortunately, if you need me the rest of the night, you'll have to contact me through the CB radio," I announce, updating the local emergency services dispatcher.

"You're always forgetting something," she teases me.

I groan, not in the mood for joking around tonight. I heave a sigh and plead, "Not tonight, Lucy. It's already been a really long night and this storm has barely begun."

"Got it, Max," she acknowledges, instantly stifling her amusement at my expense. "I'll also let the cleanup crew know you have to drop the cars on the back of the truck at the shop first. Then you'll be able to make it there to tow all three cars out of there."

"Thanks," I grumble. "It shouldn't take me too long to finish up. I have to go deal with Mr. and Mrs. Lawrence, now," I inform her with another sigh of exhaustion.

"Okay, good luck," she offers.

"Thanks," I repeat.

"And Max," she says, to get my attention.

"Yeah?" I question.

"I'm really glad you're here helping out your dad. This storm would be a lot on anyone," she alerts me.

I grimace at her compliment; thankful she can't see my reaction. I'm grateful I'm here helping out my family too, but not for the same reasons she thinks. My stomach flips anxiously at just the thought of everything that's happened this past year. It's still hard for me to process sometimes. I clear my throat and square my shoulders, even though she can't see me. Then I force a blunt reply, "Yup. Gotta' go. Bye." I disconnect the call before she can say anything else.

I toss my phone into the console, knowing it's probably done for the night without a charge. I don't have a cord on me and I don't want to waste time going to get one. I groan and run my hands through my short, dark brown, wavy hair and zip up my brown winter coat before stepping back out into the cold and snow. I quickly climb out of the truck and shut the door behind me. I stuff my hands into my coat pockets as the wind blows harshly down on me, swirling snow all around me and giving me a chill. I trudge to the front of a black Ford pick-up truck only two or three years old. I knock lightly on the window of the driver's side door. Mr. Lawrence lowers the window, his whole body filled with tension. "Alright," I begin, "I have Mrs. Lawrence's SUV all locked in. I'll drop it off at my dad's shop, right now," I inform them.

"When will he be able to take a look at it?" he inquires.

I sigh and shrug apologetically in response. "I'm honestly not sure. The shop is pretty full already. Plus, with this weather," I remind him, gesturing towards our surroundings, "it may be a while."

"But we were supposed to go visit my sister and her family for the holidays," Mrs. Lawrence complains. "How are we supposed to get up there and bring all the Christmas presents with us in this thing?" she ponders. Then she gestures to the pick-up truck they're sitting in.

I arch my eyebrows in challenge, fighting a smile. "Looks like this truck has plenty of room," I tell her, not even bothering to look anywhere except at her.

"Not inside the cab," she insists.

I sigh in exasperation and make an effort not to roll my eyes. I'm not sure what she expects me to do. I repeat, "I'm sorry, but I don't know what else to tell you, Mrs. Lawrence. Either way, I can't do anything except tow your car to my dad's shop and tell him you need it back as soon as he's able to get it done. I wish I could do more to help you out," I add, forcing a smile.

She crosses her arms over her chest in frustration and reluctantly mumbles, "Fine. Thank you, Max."

I give her a firm nod in response. Then Mr. Lawrence repeats her statement, sounding happier than Mrs. Lawrence or myself with the outcome, "Thanks, Max."

I nod in acknowledgement, before telling them both, "Merry Christmas." Then, I take a step back, away from their truck.

"Merry Christmas!" they both call back.

Just before Mr. Lawrence closes the window completely, I hear him grumble, "I told you, you shouldn't be on the roads in this weather, but you're out here trying to go Christmas shopping."

I chuckle to myself and shake my head as I hurry back to my tow truck. I climb into the cab, pulling the door shut behind me. I drop my head against the steering wheel in annoyance. I don't understand why everyone always acts like either the weather or the accidents themselves are my fault. Believe me, this is not the way I want to spend my night. I give myself a slight shake and pick up my phone, noticing it's only at 3%. "That won't last long," I mumble to myself.

My phone beeps, while I'm still holding it and a text message from one of my former coworkers in the city pops up. I hesitate, knowing it can't be that important right now. Besides, it's probably not something I want to see. Plus, my phone is practically running on empty, I should leave it alone in case I do have an important phone call or something, instead of allowing my morose curiosity to take over. I clench my jaw and attempt to ignore it.

Not even a minute later, I ignore my own warning and open the attachment. I click on the included link regarding an article that was just released about the company. I read the title, "Bare named new COO," instantly causing my whole body to go rigid. My phone suddenly dies and turns itself off before I have the chance to read anything further. I glare at my phone and toss it a little harder than necessary, into the console with a grunt of frustration. I try to shake it off, but I'm definitely not successful. My whole body feels stiff just thinking about Bare getting the promotion that was supposed to be mine. It's not like I would ever want to go back, or even change a single one of my decisions. I needed to be here with my family. I wanted to be here. I still do, but that doesn't mean I want to see someone else take my place.

I exhale harshly and run my fingers through my hair in frustration. I slowly pull back out onto the snowy streets. I turn the tow truck around and start the short drive back to town and my dad's shop, towing a car on the bottom and Mrs. Lawrence's SUV on the top. I can't believe how many accidents there have been tonight. Sure, the weather is terrible, but shouldn't that be a good reason to stay home instead of venturing out? I already feel like I've been driving all night to pull cars out of the snow, but with this storm, I'm sure my night has just begun. Although, I have to admit, I am pretty comfortable up here in our new tow truck and I love the American Flag Design my dad picked out to cover the front of the truck.

I guess the good news for me is, after this storm, most people won't have much of a choice, but to stay where they are and hopefully they won't be out traveling on Christmas. Which means, we should finally be able to have a nice family Christmas this year, without the swinging door of friends, family, neighbors and even strangers going in and out. After the tough year we've had, I not only think we need a relaxing holiday like that, I also believe we deserve it.

Flashing hazard lights up ahead, catch my attention, disrupting my thoughts. I exhale a harsh sigh. "There's another one," I grumble to myself. I pull over to the side of the road and put my truck in park. I flip my flashers on to warn other drivers that we're here. Then I shine my headlights onto the car and immediately notice the out of state license plate. I don't have room for another anything on my truck right now, but I still have to make sure whomever was in the car is okay, if they're still here. I brace myself for the cold as I jump out of the cab and lumber towards what I think is a light blue car. It's honestly hard to tell under all that snow. I glance up towards the night sky as I approach, thankful the snow has temporarily let up. I quickly scan the exterior of the car from front to back, noticing two flat tires. I move closer to the driver's side window to check if anyone is still inside. I instantly spot a platinum blonde head of hair leaning up against the window. I chuckle to myself and knock lightly on the glass.

The woman startles and spins towards me in her seat. Her tired blue-grey eyes connect with my green ones, promptly knocking the breath from my lungs. I see the instantaneous relief reflected in her eyes, before she scrambles to step out of her car. She closes the door behind her and exclaims, "Oh, thank goodness you found me!"

I can't help but notice how beautiful she is, with her high cheekbones, big, blue eyes, accented with long eyelashes and a petite frame. She seems so small next to my 5'11" height, probably about five inches shorter than me. "Are you okay?" I inquire, concerned.

"Yes," she sighs, "but my car is stuck. I have a flat," she informs me. She gestures to her car behind her, full of regret.

I can't hide my smirk, loving that she just stated the obvious. I nod my head in confirmation and correct her statement. "You have two flats. What happened?" I question, curiously.

I notice a slight flinch. Then she tilts her head down, looking away from my gaze as her cheeks turn a pretty shade of pink, from more than just the cold. She finally opens her mouth to answer, obviously a little uncomfortable. "It's stupid," she mumbles.

I nod in agreement, still trying to hold back my smile. "Probably," I confirm, "seeing as you're driving into the biggest snowstorm of the decade." She narrows her eyes at me and I attempt to school my expression before I try again. "So, what happened?" I repeat.

She takes a deep breath and purses her lips, as if she's not sure if she wants to tell me the truth. I remain quiet, waiting for her reply. She finally blurts out, "I skidded." Then she looks up at me from under her lashes, as if she's expecting me to say something about her response.

I pause and take a moment to look at the ground around me, trying to tell if I missed something, or maybe the snow covered up something from earlier if she's been here for a while, but no luck. I bite the inside of my cheek, trying to fight another smirk, as I realize why she looks so anxious. I arch my eyebrows in challenge and reveal, "I don't see any skid marks."

She sighs in defeat, her shoulders instantly sagging. "Fine!" she hisses through her teeth, as if I did something to cause her accident. She's just like every other driver tonight, the thought making me grimace. "I was looking for my phone and I took my eyes off the road," she admits. "I swerved to avoid a car and I landed in the ditch," she explains. "Happy?" she probes, accusingly.

I can't hide my grin any longer, as I stare at her in amusement. It's not too often I get such an honest admission. So many people will continue to deny the truth when I ask them questions, even when I know the story they're telling me is impossible. Instead of commenting further on the accident, I prompt, "How long have you been out here?"

She shrugs and huffs in frustration, although I'm honestly not sure if it's with me, or because of her situation. "I don't know," she admits. "What time is it?" she inquires.

I briefly glance at the black and silver watch on my left wrist to check the time. "Almost eight-thirty," I inform her.

Her eyes widen even more, causing them to appear even more beautiful. "Eight-thirty?" she repeats, shocked. "No! That can't be right," she argues, sounding a little panicked.

I arch my eyebrows in surprise at her reaction. "Well, it is," I confirm. "Are you supposed to be somewhere?" I prod.

"Yes!" she declares, irritably. "Home! For Christmas," she explains.

I nod my head in understanding and question, "Where's home? I can give you a ride," I offer.

"Outside of Boston," she states.

I huff a laugh of disbelief. "Boston?" I reiterate. She nods in confirmation. "You're a far way from home, Princess," I proclaim.

Her eyes narrow and she glares at me. "Don't call me Princess," she grumbles, obviously getting annoyed with me.

I shake my head and hold my hands up slightly in surrender. "I didn't mean anything by it," I insist. The last thing I need is to get into an argument with a beautiful woman on the side of the road right now.

"My name is Ivy," she informs me.

My eyebrows draw together in confusion and I prompt, "And?"

She pinches her lips tightly together and takes a deep breath before responding. "Can you get me to Boston?" she asks, impatiently.

I laugh out loud at her question. I can't help it. It's been such a long night already and she wants me to drive her to Boston during a snowstorm? She may be beautiful, but she's obviously not thinking straight. "No," I finally answer.

"Why not?" she demands, appearing confused.

Maybe the Princess nickname really does suit her perfectly. I arch my eyebrows, astonished at her gumption. "Boston is a six hour drive in good weather," I emphasize, "and we're in the middle of a snowstorm," I remind her. I hold out my arms, gesturing to the snow all around us and give her a look, letting her know exactly what I think of her request.

She looks around before focusing back on me. She crosses her arms over her chest and gives me a defiant look in challenge. Then she points out the obvious, again. "It stopped snowing," she broadcasts.

I bite my tongue, reminding myself not to say anything I might regret. A short fuse will not help me make it through tonight. "Not for long. It's going to start up again soon," I announce.

She glares at me before sighing in defeat. "Well, can you tow me somewhere?" she requests, gesturing towards my truck.

I nod in confirmation. "I can get your car to my dad's shop, but you're going to have to wait a while," I inform her, matter of fact.

"Why?" she challenges, perplexed.

"Because I'm already full-up," I explain. I gesture towards the back of the tow-truck and release a sigh of utter exhaustion.

"So why did you stop?" she questions, her frustration obviously growing.

I grit my teeth and attempt to hold back my increasing annoyance with this woman before answering her. "To make sure you were alive," I state, barely able to believe she's asking.

She crosses her arms over her chest and pops her hip out as she narrows her eyes even further. "How kind of you," she grumbles, sarcastically.

I clench my jaw in irritation. This woman is about to push my patience to its limits and I don't even know her. I force myself to take a deep, calming breath before I open my mouth. "Listen, Princess, I can leave you here or drop you off at the inn," I inform her. "It's your call," I declare, like it doesn't matter to me either way.

She stares at me in shock. I return her glower, refusing to back down. What does she expect me to do? She finally breaks our stare and drops her arms to her sides as she huffs in aggravation. "I'll get my stuff," she gripes, as if I'm inconveniencing her.

I take another deep breath, trying to calm myself down, before I'm stuck in my cab alone with her on the ride into town. I watch as she slips behind the wheel of her car and grabs her keys out of the ignition. I turn towards my truck and make it three steps before she stops me on the way to the trunk of her car. "Aren't you going to help me with my bag?" she queries, incredulously.

I slowly spin back towards her, just before I reach my door. I know I should do exactly that, but for some reason, I want to do the exact opposite. It's not like I'll ever see her again, anyway. I tilt my head to the side and remind her, "You got it in there yourself. I'm sure you can handle it."

Her mouth drops open in pure shock. I turn back towards my truck, amused and smirking to myself at the look on her face. She's feisty when she's mad. I climb up behind the wheel and watch as she heaves her suitcase out of the trunk of her car and strides towards me, struggling to pull it behind her through the deepening snow. Although, my mom wouldn't be happy with me, I have a strong urge to push her even more. Instead of doing what I know I should, I roll down my window and lean my head outside. "You coming?" I yell out the window. She freezes and glares up at me before she continues towards me, practically stomping the rest of the way to the truck. I chuckle as I watch her, completely entertained. She yanks the passenger door open and then heaves her suitcase up into the cab of my truck, before she shoves it behind the seat. She climbs up into the cab and closes the door behind her with a grunt.

"Good job," I praise her, with a forced smile.

I watch her lips thin, as she pretends to ignore my comment. "Do you have a phone I could use?" she requests.

I shake my head and fight a smile, knowing she won't like what I'm about to say. "Nope," I reveal. "It ran out of juice about an hour ago."

She grimaces and immediately buckles her seatbelt. "Fantastic," she grumbles. "Let's just go," she concedes, sounding defeated.

I nod in agreement, feeling a little bad for the dejected look on her face. "You got it, Princess," I concur. She clenches her jaw and folds her arms angrily over her chest, staring straight ahead. I turn towards the road and chuckle to myself, attempting to push my guilty feelings away, as I put the truck into gear.

We make it to the inn without running into any other accidents or stranded cars on the side of the road. I park the truck near the front entrance of the inn, decorated brightly, but classically for Christmas. I turn towards her and watch her face soften as she takes in the site of the white lights outlining the tan brick building, enhanced with garland and red bows. White wooden reindeer, all with a red bow and bells around their necks, rest on the lawn, now white from the freshly fallen snow, to the right of the front door. When she finally glances in my direction, her beauty takes my breath away with her softened features. I square my shoulders and close myself off, feeling like I need to protect myself from her, but I'm not sure why. I gesture towards the front door of the inn, decorated with a large Christmas wreath covered with pinecones, white lights and a thick, red velvet bow, as I paste on a fake smile. "Here you go," I announce, simply.

She purses her lips; obviously holding back from whatever she wants to say to me. She pushes the door open and starts to climb out of the truck. I watch as she begins to pull her suitcase out of the back, fumbling with the handle and her purse. She squares her shoulders and faces me before she gets it completely out. She pastes on a smile as she stares at me, probably trying to remember her manners. She takes a deep breath and says with overt, sarcastic, appreciation, "Thank you for the ride." Then she waits for my response.

I grin wide; already knowing my reply will irritate her. "You're welcome, Princess."

She purses her lips and appears to bite down on her tongue to stop herself from saying anything else to me. She heaves her suitcase the rest of the way out and jumps out of the truck, almost falling backwards into the snow. She catches herself, gripping her suitcase tightly. I watch as she walks towards the front door of the town inn and steps inside through the front door, without looking back.

I heave another sigh and run my hand through my hair, as the door closes behind her. I may have had fun pushing her buttons, but I couldn't help myself. She was absolutely beautiful, yet there was something about her I can't quite figure out. She was able to pull a strong reaction out of me way too easily, especially when I don't even know her. I shake my head at myself in annoyance, as realization dawns on me. "Why am I thinking about her like I want to ask her out?" I mumble to myself. She's not even from around here. Besides, a relationship is the last thing I need. I have too many other things to worry about. I don't need a woman around that I probably can't trust anyway.

I sigh and run my hand through my hair again, feeling a little bad for the way I acted, but it's not like I'm ever going to see her again. I immediately attempt to push thoughts of her out of my head, which is easier said than done. I put the truck back in gear and force myself to focus on the road in front of me. "It doesn't matter. She's just passing through town, anyway," I remind myself. Her plates said South Carolina and she said something about trying to get home to Boston for Christmas. Either way, neither place is anywhere close to

29

Pennsylvania. I pull away from the inn and turn the tow-truck towards my dad's shop. I need to drop the cars on back, before heading back out for more pick-ups, including Princess's car.

Chapter 3

Ivy

I stride through the front door of an adorable, little inn, dragging my suitcase behind me. I pause inside the door to take a few deep breaths, as I attempt to push thoughts of that infuriating man out of my head. He may have been gorgeous with that bright smile, underneath light stubble; let alone his sparkling emerald green eyes and his tall, lean, firm frame, but he definitely didn't have any Christmas spirit. I pinch my lips tightly together. A man that handsome would be nothing but trouble for me. Besides, I can't believe he dared to call me Princess! I'm definitely not a princess and I don't appreciate him calling me that. Hasn't my day been bad enough? Being stuck out in the middle of nowhere and needing his help does not make me a princess. I give myself another light shake, trying to pull myself out of my internal rant. I don't need to think about that man anymore. I need to stay as far away as possible from men like him. Hopefully, I never have to see him again, anyway. Until I have to pick up my car, I remind myself and scrunch my face up in aggravation. Then again, a lot of tow truck companies have nothing to do with fixing the cars they tow, but not all of them. Hopefully, I'll be lucky and we won't cross paths again while I'm stuck here.

I heave a sigh of exhaustion. I'm ready to get some sleep and try to forget about today, at least for the night. Tomorrow I'll have to deal with my car. Hopefully they'll be able to change my tires and I can be on my way. If not, I'll have to try to figure out how to make it the rest of the way home. I grimace and give myself another mental shake. "It will be fine," I murmur to myself, hoping the words will help make it true. In the meantime, I need to get in touch with my family and try to get some sleep.

I take a quick look around the small lobby of the inn. I immediately notice the inside is as beautifully decorated for Christmas as the outside. Green garland wraps around the wood paneled poles near the front desk. There's more strung loosely around the windows and doorways, in front of the desk, as well as on the wall behind it. A red berry wreath hangs high on the wall behind the clerk. Red and white stockings dangle at the top of each swoop in front of the desk; with a wooden sign in the middle I can't quite read from here. A three-foot plastic Santa statue sits in the corner, greeting everyone with a welcoming painted smile. Small poinsettia plants are placed in red or green Christmas painted planters and rest on every table in the lobby. As I approach the desk, I notice a Christmas green mailbox with a red flag raised up on one side, with the words, "letters to Santa," painted in white lettering on each side. I exhale slowly and smile to myself, feeling a little better in this cozy holiday atmosphere. I'm honestly grateful to be somewhere warm and comfortable for the night, instead of trying to stay warm in my car in the middle of nowhere. In addition, all the Christmas decorations make it feel more like home, which definitely helps improve my mood.

I stop and wait my turn in line, while I watch a lovely and sophisticated woman, who appears to be about the same age as my mom. She's standing in front of the desk talking with the tall man behind the desk, who I assume works here. He has broad shoulders and short, salt and pepper hair. He's dressed in a white button down dress shirt and gray sweater vest. The woman has straight auburn hair, cut just above her shoulders. She's dressed as if she just finished a business meeting in her tailored navy blue pantsuit, with a floral navy and cream, silk top underneath her blazer and simple matching pumps. I can't help but overhear part of their conversation, as I hesitantly approach the desk. "The snow should be done by then. Everyone can walk on over for the party, if nothing else," the woman expresses, with a bright smile.

"I'll be there with bells on, Mrs. Mayor," the desk clerk agrees. He nods and gives her a genuine grin in response.

"Quite literally, since you're playing Santa!" she exclaims, teasing him. They both laugh clearly amused.

Suddenly, the desk clerk notices me standing off to the side. He instantly straightens, squares his shoulders and turns towards me. He clears his throat as he leans his hands on the wood countertop in front of him and holds my gaze. He gives me a welcoming smile and in his deep voice politely requests, "May I help you?"

I shuffle closer to the desk, setting my suitcase to the side as the woman takes a step back. She sets her purse down by her feet and begins putting a red, wool dress coat on. I glance at the clerk's nametag and greet him by name. "Hi, George," I say and grin up at him. "I'd like a room for the night, please," I request.

He grimaces and then immediately apologizes, "Oh, I'm sorry, but there are no more rooms available."

My heart drops into my stomach with his statement. That can't be true. My mouth drops slightly open and my nerves suddenly attack my stomach, causing it to flip-flop. "Nothing at all?" I prompt, feeling my anxiety rapidly returning.

He shakes his head, his eyes apologetic, but that doesn't stop my growing panic. "No, I'm sorry," he answers.

I have no idea what I'm going to do if I don't find a place to stay soon. I don't even have my car anymore or a phone to call someone to help. What am I supposed to do? "Are there any other hotels in town?" I question, desperately.

He shakes his head and again offers me an apologetic and helpless smile. "No, there aren't," he reveals.

"What about nearby? Can I take a cab to one nearby or something?" I inquire, feeling more and more restless with every question that pops into my head. I have nowhere to go. What am I going to do? I repeat the same question in my head over and over.

He smiles sadly as he shakes his head. He regretfully clarifies, "I'm sorry, but all of the hotels in the area are completely sold out."

I sigh in defeat and grumble, "Fantastic." My stomach churns uneasily as my brain races to think of something to solve my problem, but I'm getting nowhere. I feel like my mind is on a frantic loop and coming up completely empty. I have absolutely no idea what I'm going to do. I grimace, knowing my parents aren't going to be happy with me. They already told me they didn't want me to attempt to beat the storm, but I refused to listen to them. I didn't think something like this could happen to me, especially at Christmastime. Boy, was I wrong. I keep hearing my mom's voice calling after me, as I hung up on her earlier, warning me not to drive. It's as if it's running through my head on repeat. Now I'm supposed to call them and tell them I don't have anywhere to go during this storm? That's if I'm even able to find a phone I can use to call them. They are going to be so worried about me. What else could possibly go wrong?

The same woman steps back up to the desk, now with a candy apple green scarf wrapped protectively around her neck, underneath her red coat. She reminds me of an ad for Christmas Spirit, the opposite of the tow truck driver's attitude. She stands right next to me and I notice she has a couple inches on my 5'5" height, even without her short heels. "I'm sorry to butt in," she interrupts politely, "but is something wrong?" she asks me, kindly.

I look into her warm blue eyes and see nothing but concern in them. I sigh heavily, feeling my shoulders sag, overwhelmed with my situation. "My car is stuck in a ditch and I can't get home," I concede.

"Where is home?" she inquires, her eyebrows arched in question.

"Right outside of Boston," I answer.

"Ooh, you're a long way from home," George sympathizes, repeating the same words as the tow truck driver, but laced with empathy.

I nod sadly at the reminder of how much farther I still have to go to make it home to my family. Now with this accident, I may never be able to make it home for Christmas, I grimace. "Yes, I know," I acknowledge, sadly.

"You don't have any friends in the area?" she questions, curiously.

I shake my head, unhappily, knowing she's only trying to help. "No," I deny. It would be so much easier if I did. "I was driving home from Charleston to spend Christmas with my family when my car got stuck," I explain.

Her whole face softens and floods with understanding. "Oh, you poor thing. You must be exhausted!" she exclaims.

The desk clerk, George, clears his throat to get our attention. He interrupts and informs her, "We don't have any vacancies at all, Mrs. Mayor. Everything is booked from here to Oneonta because of the storm," he emphasizes.

"Oh, no," she proclaims, obviously sympathetic to my situation. She turns back towards me, full of the kind of confidence I hope to have one day about my cooking. She smiles and announces, "You can stay at my house."

I gasp and my eyes widen in surprise at her offer. Unsure if I heard her correctly, I clarify, "Excuse me?"

"I have plenty of room for you at my house," she proclaims. "You will have your own guest room with a private bathroom," she elaborates. "It's really no trouble at all," she insists.

"Mrs. Mayor, are you sure?" George prompts. "We don't have any openings here until Christmas morning," he enlightens her.

She nods firmly and declares, "Quite. I'm not leaving this young lady out in the cold during the holidays," she insists.

I shake my head in disbelief and hold my hand to my chest, grateful for her offer, but still remember my manners. "I couldn't possibly impose on you like that," I tell her.

"Oh, please," she states, attempting to push my concern to the side. She casually waves her hand and dismisses my appreciation like its no big deal, but this is a huge deal to me. "It's no imposition at all," she repeats. "Besides," she shrugs, "If I can't show you hospitality, then who can?" she challenges, grinning. "I am the mayor of Bethlehem, after all," she announces, with a wide smile.

My lips twitch up in amusement, but I try to fight it, in an attempt to hide my laughter. "Bethlehem?" I question in surprise. I pinch my lips tightly together and arch my eyebrows in disbelief. There is no way I heard her correctly.

"Yes," she confirms with a strong nod in affirmation. "You're in Bethlehem, Pennsylvania," she announces, proudly.

A small chuckle escapes my lips and I swiftly slap my hand over my mouth, trying to stop myself from laughing, but it doesn't help. A giggle easily escapes and soon I'm laughing uncontrollably. I'm not really sure if it's because of the irony of where I am, or complete exhaustion and frustration due to the situation I've gotten myself into, but I can't stop laughing.

"What's so funny?" George prods, curiously.

I slowly catch my breath and calm myself down, before I'm able to answer him. I glance back and forth between the two of them, hoping they understand my humor and I'm not about to embarrass myself. "I'm in Bethlehem and there is no room at the Inn for Christmas!" I explain. I burst out laughing again, as soon as the words are out of my mouth.

The woman instantly joins in my laughter, followed by the clerk. When we're all able to get our hilarity under control, the woman turns back to me and encourages me. She smiles kindly, "Come on. I'll take you home."

I grin up at her appreciatively and breathe a sigh of relief, knowing I'll have somewhere warm and safe to sleep tonight. "Thank you," I tell her, gratefully. "I'm Ivy," I say. I hold out my hand for her to shake, as I introduce myself.

She takes my hand in hers and gives it a firm shake, smiling broadly. "It's very nice to meet you, Ivy," she replies, kindly. "I'm Judy," she introduces herself.

George grins and holds out his hand, gesturing towards Judy. He emphasizes, "Mayor Judy Carson, that is!"

She smiles modestly and her cheeks turn slightly pink. I breathe another sigh of relief, still grinning. The fact that I'm staying with the mayor of the town should help both of my parents relax a little bit and give them some comfort. They will definitely want to know I'm somewhere safe. She glances over at him and softly proclaims, "Thank you, George."

"You're welcome," he responds, proudly, seeming oblivious to her slight show of embarrassment.

"Spread the word to the town that the Christmas party is at my house, instead of being cancelled," she reminds him, quickly changing the subject.

My eyes widen in surprise. I'm a little overwhelmed just thinking about the idea of having a whole town over to my parents' house for any kind of get together and I love cooking for people. I adore doing dinner parties or get-togethers, but that sounds like a lot of people. I can't help but question it, my disbelief clear in the tone of my voice. "You're having a Christmas party for an entire town?"

She shrugs and grins like it's something she does every day. Then she again attempts to play off her kindness and generosity. "It's not a very big town," she emphasizes, the corners of her lips twitching up in amusement. My eyes widen and I smile to myself, already knowing she's a good person and I'm going to be just fine. She turns her attention back towards the desk and smiles at George. She waves goodbye and proclaims, "Goodnight, George."

"Goodnight, Mrs. Mayor," he grins and waves in return. "Goodbye, Miss," he offers me the same gesture.

"Goodbye. Thank you, George," I reply and return his small wave. Then I grip my suitcase tightly and spin on my heel before I trudge back towards the exit. I follow the mayor out the front door of the cozy Bethlehem Inn, dragging my suitcase behind me.

I take a deep breath, preparing myself for the cold, just as we step outside. The wind whips and whirls in powerful gusts, blowing some of the snow up into my face and causing me to flinch. "Thank you again, Judy," I reiterate, exceedingly grateful for her extreme kindness. I can't help but think she really is the complete opposite of the tow truck driver I met earlier tonight. Then again, why do I keep thinking about him? I give myself a mental shake and focus on Judy. "I honestly don't know what I would've done if you hadn't been here when I arrived," I admit. Just the thought of having nowhere to go sends chills back up my spine.

"I'm happy I'm able to help," she responds, with a kind smile. I grin back at her, more grateful to have met her, than I may ever be able to express. I breathe a sigh of relief and smile to myself, as I put my suitcase in her trunk. I have to admit, it kind of feels like she's my very own Christmas angel. I giggle and close the trunk before I make my way around to the passenger side of her small SUV and slip inside. I buckle my seatbelt as Judy starts the car.

She glances over at me and informs me, "Don't worry, I have snow tires on this thing. Plus, we only have to go about a mile to get home."

"Wonderful," I proclaim. "Thank you again, Judy," I reiterate.

She smiles at me, giving me comfort, before she faces forward and puts the car into gear. She turns towards the snow-covered roads, as I relax back into my seat.

Chapter 4

Ivy

Judy parks her car in the brick-lined, blacktop driveway and I unbuckle my seatbelt. "Here we are," she announces.

I climb out of the car and close the door behind me, as I look up in awe at a large white colonial home adorned with dark green shutters, decorated classically with white Christmas lights. I grab my suitcase out of the trunk and walk up the brick pathway leading towards the house, taking everything in as I go. An extra large Christmas wreath with a red bow hangs on the front of the house between the first and second floor windows. A smaller version of what appears to be the same wreath beautifies the front door. The large white pillars on the front porch are wrapped with a thick, red ribbon, causing them to resemble giant candy canes. A sign stating, "Santa Stops Here," enhances the bare winter garden next to the front porch, while a small choir of three white angels with gold halos sits on the grass in front of the bushes partially buried in the snow. I smirk, thinking again about how this woman has become my angel, saving me from sleeping out in the cold tonight, but I don't get a chance to tell her that before she pushes through her front door.

She steps into a large foyer with tall ceilings and wide plank mahogany floors. The stairway to the second floor is just off to my right. The banister matches the wood floors and it's decorated beautifully with thick, green garland, white lights, red ribbons and bows. To my left stands a stuffed boy and girl elf, about eighteen inches tall, dressed in various patterns of red and green. A small, half-circle, entryway table sits up against the wall near another door, with a white and silver wooden rocking horse, about ten inches tall, sitting on top. Everything is absolutely stunning and I've barely stepped into the house. I take a deep breath, the light scent of pine in the air. I clutch my suitcase as I take in my surroundings, while Judy turns and pushes the front door closed behind me.

"Charles?" Judy calls, her voice echoing throughout the house. "I'm home!" she declares, with a smile in her voice.

A man just over six feet tall enters from the kitchen. He has the sleeves of his red, black and gray plaid shirt rolled up to his elbows and the bottom untucked, hanging over his dark blue jeans. He's tall and thin with broad shoulders. He has perfectly coifed gray hair and friendly blue-grey eyes. "Hi, Honey," he says, greeting her sweetly. He immediately closes the distance between them and presses his lips to hers in a chaste welcome home kiss.

"We have company tonight," Judy announces. She glances over to acknowledge me. Then she adds, "And maybe for the next few days."

"Oh?" he asks, seeming more curious than anything.

Judy turns to me and introduces us as she removes her gloves and coat. "Ivy, this is my husband, Charles."

Charles holds his hand out for me to shake and I slip my hand into his. "It's nice to meet you," he states, with a gentle smile.

I grin and release his hand. "It's nice to meet you too, Charles. Thank you so much for your hospitality."

Charles grins broadly, as if he himself invited me to stay. "You're welcome," he replies. I smile at the way he responds, as if he's not surprised I'm standing in his

41

foyer with a suitcase. It makes me wonder if things like this happen here very often.

"Ivy's car is in a ditch outside of town," Judy informs him.

His eyebrows immediately draw down in concern. He turns to me and questions "Are you all right?"

I nod my head and smile appreciatively up at him. "Yes, thanks. I'm just tired," I admit, with a small shrug.

"There's no room at the Inn, so I said she can stay with us until the storm passes," Judy explains to her husband.

"Of course!" he instantly agrees.

I grimace, realizing how long it's been since I spoke with my parents. "May I please use your phone?" I ask, suddenly anxious. "My family must be worried sick about me. I lost my phone earlier today and I haven't talked to them in hours," I rationalize.

Judy nods in agreement, "Absolutely. It's in the kitchen on the counter." She points in the same direction Charles just came from. "We'll give you some privacy to talk to them."

"Use it whenever you want while you're here," Charles offers.

"Thank you so much," I tell them both, appreciatively. I walk towards the kitchen and immediately find the phone on the counter. I pick it up and almost have to remind myself of the number out loud as I dial. I'm so used to just pressing a button on my cell phone screen to connect me to anyone, even my family. I rarely have to think about it, except when I'm filling out forms. I pull the phone up to my ear and wait for someone to pick up.

"Hello?" the warm, soft voice of my mother drifts over the line, instantly giving me comfort. My mom is a beautiful, bubbly woman with a great sense of humor.

She has straight, brown hair cut just above her shoulders, big, warm, brown eyes and a contagious smile. I definitely got my height and petite build from my mom, but I'm taller than her by an inch.

"Mom?" I prompt, feeling the emotions from the day welling up inside me. I pause and then I breathe an audible sigh of relief before I continue. "Mom, it's me, Ivy," I announce, a small smile on my face.

"Ivy!" she exclaims, relief evident in the sound of her voice. "Ivy, we've been worried sick about you!" she declares, vehemently.

I smile wider feeling so much better, just being able to talk to them. I imagine my dad has been pacing near the phone all evening. He's a big man at 6'4" with an extremely broad build. He has brown eyes and usually wears dark rimmed glasses. He's bald on top with short salt and pepper hair in the back, as well as in his short, neatly trimmed beard and mustache. "I know, Mom. I'm sorry," I apologize, sincerely. "I lost my phone when I stopped to get something to eat," I explain. "I'm fine though. Everything is fine," I emphasize, knowing they worry about me.

I hear dad whispering loudly near the phone. "Ask her where she is," he requests, anxiously. Then he pauses before he questions louder into the phone, "Ivy, where are you?"

"Bill, stop it," she demands, scolding my dad before she speaks into the phone again. "Ivy, where are you?" she repeats.

I hear my twin brother, Sawyer, in the background, making my smile grow even more. "Ivy's on the phone?" he inquires. Sawyer is not only my twin brother, but he's also my best friend. We may tease each other endlessly, but we always watch out for one another. He's just a little taller than me, with a lean build, light brown hair and brown eyes. I wish I were there with them, but at least I'm no longer out in the cold.

"I'm in Bethlehem, Pennsylvania. I'm staying with the Mayor and her family because there was no room at the inn," I reveal. I giggle to myself, still amused when I repeat the words aloud.

Mom chuckles, appreciating the irony of the situation, like me. I hear dad ask, "What's so funny, Mary?"

"Ivy is staying at the mayor's house in Bethlehem because there was no room at the inn," she explains, and then giggles again.

"That's not funny, Mary," dad insists.

"Mom, come on," Sawyer adds, sounding exasperated.

Mom laughs again, then stops. "Sorry," she says. I really am so much like my mom. She takes a deep breath to calm down before she continues. "The roads are really bad here, Ivy. Just spend the night there and maybe you will be able to leave tomorrow," she suggests.

"There's an even bigger storm coming tomorrow!" dad exclaims.

"I knew she wasn't going to make it," Sawyer complains, making me wince.

"Let's see what happens with the weather, okay?" mom proposes. She always pushes to remain positive for us in any situation and this is obviously no different.

I sigh in defeat, remembering my car. "Yeah," I agree. I hesitate before adding, "And I need to see what's going on with my car, too. Don't worry, I'm fine," I emphasize, "but there might be a little issue with the car," I enlighten them, barely containing my wince.

"Your car?" mom repeats, the worry instantly returning to her voice. "What's wrong with your car? Did something happen?" she blurts out, anxiously.

"Is she okay?" Sawyer questions.

"Did she get into an accident?" dad yells.

"It's no big deal," I attempt to accentuate. "I got a flat. I need to get it fixed before I drive my car again," I apprise them. "I'll call you tomorrow. I love you, Mom!"

"I love you, too, Ivy," mom proclaims, affectionately.

"Love you, Ives," Sawyer yells.

"Love you, Honey," dad calls.

I smile to myself as their terms of endearment sound out through the phone, warming my heart. "Tell Daddy and Sawyer I love them too. Bye!"

"Bye, Ivy," mom states just before I hang up the phone.

I walk back into the foyer to find my suitcase and Charles gone. "Did you get a hold of your parents?" Judy inquires.

I nod in confirmation and force a smile. "I sure did. Thank you," I tell her, softly.

"Charles brought your suitcase up to your room," she informs me.

"Thank you so much," I respond, gratefully.

"You're welcome," she replies. "We own the auto body shop in town. Charles will take a look at your car when the storm lets up," she announces.

"Oh, that would be wonderful! The tow truck driver said he was going to go back and get my car," I advise.

She arches her eyebrows in surprise and something else I can't quite decipher. She prompts, "You met Max?"

I shrug, "If that's the tow truck driver's name, then yes. He dropped me off at the inn," I inform her.

"Really?" she pushes, her eyes wide with curiosity.

I nod in confirmation, "Yes. He said he was going to get my car, but with everything that happened, I can't remember what shop he said he would bring it to," I admit. I do remember he gave me a card with the phone number for the shop.

"Ours," Judy grins, proudly. "Charles runs the only auto shop in town. He'll take a look at it for you tomorrow."

"Thank you so much, Judy. Truly," I emphasize. Knowing Charles is taking care of my car lifts a huge weight off my shoulders. Maybe I won't have to see the tow-truck driver again. My heart clenches as if it were being squeezed at the thought, but that doesn't make sense. I don't want to see him again. "That's a good thing," I mumble, reiterating the point to myself, in an attempt to convince myself it's true.

She waves a hand, dismissing me. "Stop thanking me. It's the time of year for giving, isn't it?" she questions.

I exhale gradually as a genuine smile slowly encompasses my face. I nod in agreement and reply, "Yes, I suppose it is."

"Come on, Ivy," Judy waves a hand towards the stairs. "I'll bring you up to your room," she offers.

I nod and follow Judy upstairs to the spare bedroom, the first door on the right. I walk into a nice size room with a large queen size bed filled with pillows, including red Christmas ones. Small silver reindeer sit atop a long cherry dresser with red bows. A larger red bow sits at the top of the matching headboard and silver glittered snowflakes accessorize the sides. "Here you go! Home, sweet home," Judy announces. "Well, for the time being, anyway," she adds, grinning.

"You really have a beautiful home," I compliment.

"Thank you," she replies.

Charles walks in holding a small stack of towels. "Here you go," he offers, placing them on the foot of the bed.

"Thanks," I respond.

Charles motions to the door on the left against the opposite wall from the bed and informs me, "This bathroom is all yours."

"Wonderful. Thanks," I repeat.

"You'll find new soap, shampoo and whatever else you may need under the sink in there," she advises me.

"Great," I say.

"Are you hungry?" Charles asks.

I shake my head, "No. I'm just really tired."

"We won't disturb you anymore, Ivy. Get some rest," she suggests.

"If you need anything else, just holler," Charles reminds me.

"I will. Thank you," I repeat.

"Good night," Charles says and offers a small wave.

"Good night," I reply.

I watch Charles walk out the door with Judy right behind him, but she pauses in the doorway and turns back to me. "You know," she begins, "I always say that everything happens for a reason," she announces, her eyes twinkling.

I huff a laugh and reveal, "So does my mom."

Judy's eyes sparkle even more as she responds. "Smart woman," she proclaims. She winks and continues, "I'm looking forward to finding out the reason for all of this." She grins broadly, as if she knows something I don't. "Good night, Ivy." She walks out of the room and closes the door behind her.

"I'm wondering what the reason is too," I murmur to myself. Well, there's no point in worrying about it now. I pull my suitcase up onto the bed with a groan, feeling completely exhausted. I quickly flip it open and pull out my Christmas pajamas. I may not be home, but I can still follow our traditions.

It has been such a long day. It's hard to believe this morning I was in Charleston and now I'm in Bethlehem, Pennsylvania. This was never one of the places I thought I'd be at the end of the day today. I giggle in disbelief, as I grab my bathroom bag, along with my pajamas. Then, I turn and stride to the connecting bathroom to get ready for bed. I don't want to do anything right now, except sleep.

Chapter 5

Max

I have to push myself to continue moving. I keep reminding myself my extended day and night is almost over, I just need to make it a little further. I walk through the front door of the inn completely exhausted, definitely ready to go home and get some sleep, but I have to take care of one more thing first. I found a cell phone in my truck after I dropped off the last car I towed to the shop. About the same time, George left me a message saying one of his guests lost their phone when I was helping them out with their car. I uncovered a phone earlier underneath the passenger seat of the cab, so now I'm making the effort to drive a little out of the way to drop it off for them. "Morning, George," I greet him with a sigh and a tired smile.

"Good morning," he welcomes me with a friendly grin. "Looks like you had a long night," he observes, stating the obvious.

"You could say that," I reply. "I'm sure it will be a long day, too," I concede. He nods in understanding as I hand him the cell phone. "I believe this is what your guest is looking for," I declare.

"Thank you for dropping this off," he tells me as he takes the phone. I nod my head and turn back for the door. "Tell your mom thank you, again, too," he adds.

I stop and spin back towards him, my eyebrows drawn together in confusion. "For what?" I inquire. She's always doing something to help someone out. I wonder what it was this time.

"For taking someone in who was stranded here from the snowstorm. We don't have anymore rooms available and she stepped in and helped out," he reveals, grinning proudly.

My mouth drops open in shock and my heart begins racing. "What?" I croak. I'm instantly flooded with panicked, but I don't give him a chance to answer me. I spin towards the front door and quickly run outside as if I were being chased. I sprint up to my truck and jump in behind the wheel. I buckle my seat belt and start the truck. I clench the steering wheel so tight, my knuckles begin turning white as I back out. I turn onto the main road and drive home as fast as I can, which unfortunately, is not too fast with all this snow. Luckily, we live in town and I'm able to get home relatively quick, without anything else going wrong.

I push through the front door, storming into the house and then slamming the door behind me. I can't believe mom would let another stranger into our home. "Mom! Dad?" I yell, not at all caring whom I disturb. I fly up the stairs two at a time. "Mom?" I repeat, calling out anxiously.

Mom steps out from her bedroom, wrapping her red silky robe around her, with my dad following right behind her, tying his thick cream robe at the waist. My heart slows slightly, just seeing them both safe, but my unease still remains high. "Shhh!!! Our guest is sleeping," mom emphasizes in a harsh whisper. She puts her finger to her lips and gives me a look of warning, trying to get me to quiet down.

"Guest? Mom! What were you thinking?" I ask, clearly exasperated. "He's not a guest; He's a stranger!" I yell.

"Keep your voice down," dad stresses, quiet, but firm.

"I bet he robbed you blind!" I continue ranting, ignoring both of their pleas. "Where is he?" I ask, demanding an answer.

Mom's eyebrows draw down in confusion, but her reaction doesn't immediately register in my frantic state. She inquires, "He?"

"Is he in here?" I question, urgently searching for an answer. I gesture to the guest room door right behind me.

Dad probes, "Who?" I glance at him and realize he doesn't seem to know what I'm talking about. Did she not even tell dad she brought some stranger into our home last night?

I tightly grip the handle of the bedroom door and fling it open, pushing my way into the room. "Him!" I yell. I turn to look in the direction I'm pointing. My eyes widen and my heart drops to the bottom of my stomach. I freeze and gasp at the sight in front of me. The beautiful woman who I found stuck on the side of the road last night, stands in front of me in cream onesie pajamas, with dark Christmas green cuffs. They're decorated all over with Christmas trees and reindeer. Then in the back she has a dark green-buttoned flap that reads, "No Peeking!" Her blonde hair is piled up on top of her head in a bun, messy from sleep. Her tired eyes widen in shock the moment she realizes she's not dreaming and I'm standing in front of her. She obviously recognizes me.

"You!" she yells, accusingly, instantly startling me into motion.

I suddenly realize I'm staring and move to cover my eyes, as my whole face turns bright red with embarrassment. "Oh, jeez, I'm so sorry. I didn't know," I ramble. I quickly attempt to fumble my way out of the room without looking back in her direction.

"Close the door!" she shrieks. I swiftly pull the door shut with a sick feeling in my gut. I can't believe I did that. I feel terrible for barging in on her. I finally drop my hand from my eyes with a groan of frustration.

My mom crosses her arms over her chest and narrows her eyes, glaring at me. "You have a lot of explaining to do, Maximilian," she scolds, causing me to flinch.

"I'm sorry," I grumble.

"We'll meet you in the kitchen in a few minutes," she informs me, leaving no room for argument. She gives me a pointed look, causing me to wince, before she stalks away.

I sigh heavily as I trudge downstairs. I feel like I'm five years old again and about to be scolded, but whatever my mom has to say isn't going to make me feel any worse than I already do for storming through that door. I stride into the kitchen and start a pot of coffee before I sit down at the counter and drop my head into my hands. I can't believe she's the one my mom invited to stay here. I thought I'd never see her again and now she's staying in my house? I really don't need this right now. Haven't we had enough to deal with lately?

My parents walk into the kitchen together, both dressed for the day. Dad is wearing his regular work clothes, blue jeans, grey t-shirt, green and grey flannel and his brown work boots, while my mom is dressed in navy pants, a navy knit shirt, stopping just below her elbows and a gold, cream and navy designed scarf tied at her neck. She walks over to the other side of the kitchen island, while dad takes the seat on the bar stool next to me at the counter. They both pause and wait for me to meet their gaze. I finally lift my head further and glance back and forth between both of them. I regretfully repeat, "I'm sorry." I'm not really sure what else I can say. It's obvious I made a mistake. I don't know what to do besides apologize.

"It's not us you should be apologizing to," mom reminds me, sternly. I flinch in response. She's right, but I don't know if I can. She already thinks I'm a jerk for how I acted last night. She probably wouldn't believe me if I tried.

"Why did you think there was a man here anyway?" dad questions.

I shake my head in annoyance with myself. I heave a heavy sigh and run my hands through my hair, giving the ends a light tug in frustration. I ask irritably, "Does it matter?" Both my parents give me a look of disapproval, making me wish even more that I waited to hear the rest of what George had to say. "I guess I only heard part of the story," I finally admit, with a defeated sigh.

"Max," dad mutters my name, laced with disappointment, as he exhales. I gulp down the lump in my throat, hating that tone, even though I know I deserve it. He gives a slight shake of his head, causing me to feel even worse. The look they're both giving me right now is truly painful. It's the same one I always dreaded as a kid and would do nearly anything to avoid.

"You could've texted me to give me a heads up," I remind them.

"I did," mom, claims, causing me to wince again. I forgot my phone died last night and I never took the time to charge it. "Apologize to her," mom insists. Then she turns towards the refrigerator and begins removing items for breakfast. I pour some orange juice for dad and myself, along with coffee for both of us. Then I sip my coffee too tired to do much else. I watch as mom cooks us a frittata and toasts fresh bagels. She fills a plate for both dad and me without a word.

"Thanks," I mumble, uncomfortable with the silence.

My whole body suddenly tenses, becoming aware, as I feel the atmosphere change. I don't even have to look up to know she's in the room. "Good morning," she says, both sweetly and a little bit timid as well. I glance up to find her looking at my mom. I quickly let my eyes roll over her from head to toe before she notices. She's wearing worn, form-fitting, skinny jeans and a light teal green sweater, with her hair pulled back in a French braid, hanging over her left shoulder, similar to yesterday. She looks even more beautiful than she did when I first saw her.

"Good morning, Ivy. Would you like some coffee?" my mom offers, cheerfully. I tear my gaze away from her, before I get caught and stare down at the food in front of me.

"Please," she requests.

"Have a seat," dad offers, gesturing to the seat beside him and across from me.

I take a sip of my juice, attempting to look anywhere, but at her. "Would you like breakfast?" my mom inquires.

"Sure, breakfast sounds great," Ivy agrees.

"What would you like?" she queries, as if we don't already have a buffet of food on the counter.

"I'm happy with anything, Judy. Really, I'm not picky," she insists, with a side-eye glance in my direction.

My mom nods and smiles at her, "Okay, I'll fix you a plate." She sets the coffee in front of Ivy and turns to walk back to the stove. She nudges me with her hip on the way, attempting to urge me to open my mouth.

I glance up at Ivy, guiltily. "Hi," I murmur.

"Hi," Ivy replies, timidly. I quickly focus back on my plate, like I'm a little kid with a crush and I'm getting in trouble for pulling her hair.

I feel my dad's eyes boring into me. I know I should say something before he does, but I take a bite of my eggs instead. "Max, aren't you going to say anything else?" my dad prompts.

I glance up at my dad and back at Ivy, feeling slightly remorseful. I open my mouth, intending to apologize. But when my eyes meet her questioning blue ones, an image of walking in on her this morning flashes in front of me. I can't stop the sly smile from spreading across my face. "Nice pajamas," I comment, attempting to hide my laughter as her eyes spark in annoyance.

My mom whips around with wide eyes and the spatula in her hand. She points it at me and yells my name, "Max!"

"What?" I ask, innocently.

I watch as Ivy's face gradually turns red and her eyes change from anger to embarrassment. She swallows hard and slowly rises. She clears her throat and rasps, "I'm suddenly not very hungry anymore."

I arch my eyebrows, surprised at her response. "Oh, come on, Princess. I was just teasing," I claim, defensively.

Ivy glares at me and reiterates, "I told you not to call me that!"

"You two know each other?" my dad interrupts, slightly confused.

"We met last night," Ivy concedes, with a stiff nod of her head.

"I picked her up on the side of the road and left her at the Inn," I elaborate, still feeling slightly annoyed with her.

Ivy's mouth drops open in shock and she immediately attempts to defend herself. "Not like that," she yells, continuing to glare at me.

"Don't be rude, Max," my mom instructs, sounding both surprised and completely exasperated with me. I don't blame her, but I can't seem to help myself.

"I had car trouble and Max helped me," Ivy clarifies.

"I know dear," my mom murmurs, sympathetically. "You told me," she adds, indicating she doesn't need to explain herself to us.

I cross my arms over my chest and stare at her defiantly. "You were sleeping in your car," I remind her.

"So? I lost my phone," she argues.

"You were in a ditch!" I emphasize, my voice beginning to escalate.

"I skidded and couldn't stop!" she yells back at me.

I huff a humorless laugh. "No kidding," I grumble, sarcastically.

"What is that supposed to mean?" she challenges, irritably.

"Taking your eyes off the road to look for your phone?" I probe, accusingly. "You were asking for an accident!" I proclaim.

"Max!" my mom gasps my name, shocked by my rant.

"How dare you!" Ivy yells. My stomach churns with regret as I take in her reaction. Her face is red and she appears angry, embarrassed and maybe even a little hurt.

"Why were you driving in a snowstorm anyway?" I challenge, pushing her a little more.

"I don't have to explain myself to you," she insists. She glares at me and crosses her arms over her chest, defiantly.

"Max, what has come over you?" my mom questions, clearly disappointed in me.

I open my mouth to defend my actions, when movement from my dad causes me to snap it shut. "That's enough!" my dad yells, startling me and drawing all of our attention to him. He rarely raises his voice for anything, so him doing so now, definitely shocks me, even with my current attitude. He takes a deep breath, before he continues. "Max, you're tired. Go to sleep," he asserts, firmly.

"But," I open my mouth to argue, even though I have no idea what I'm going to say.

My dad instantly interrupts me. "You've been working all night," he emphasizes. "Sleep. Now," he sternly, commands.

I grunt in annoyance, but I know I'm on the losing end of this argument. I grumble, "Yes, Sir." I push up from my seat at the counter and cast one more look at Ivy, before I turn and stalk away. I feel all of their eyes on me as I leave the room. I move towards the stairs, but change direction at the last second.

I walk through the mudroom, past our coats and shoes. Then I push through the door and stride into the garage, immediately closing it softly behind me. I instantly notice more Christmas decorations sitting on the white metal shelves mounted on the wall. I'm sure I'll be helping with those later. I sigh heavily as I sit down on the wooden steps, needing to calm myself down a little, before I go up to my room. I can't sleep when I'm this worked up, no matter how tired I am.

I groan and run my hand through my hair in annoyance, before I drop my elbows to my knees, and rest my arms there. "What is that girl even doing here?" I grumble to myself. And why is she driving me so crazy? It's like she's pushing my buttons without even trying, so of course I can't help, but push back. I drop my chin to my chest, trying to figure out how I can keep myself calm around this girl for however long she's stuck here. I just hope it's not for very long.

Chapter 6

Ivy

I watch Max stalk out of the room; still in the same clothes he was wearing when he picked me up by the side of the road. I grimace, as I realize how tired he must be after towing cars all night in the middle of a snowstorm. He definitely looks much more exhausted this morning than he did last night. I don't really blame him, which only succeeds in making me feel bad for him. Could that really be why he doesn't seem to like me? I'm honestly not sure. But if that's not it, I don't know what I could've done to offend him so much. I may have said a few ridiculous things, like asking him to drive me to Boston in this weather, but I was stressed too. The way he talks to me though, definitely makes it feel like he has something against me. I just can't figure out what it is. I pinch my lips tightly together, hating this insecure feeling I have around him, but I really don't understand the looks he gives me.

The moment he walks into a room, I feel my defenses instantly go up. Then again, I guess Max was right when he said I shouldn't have tried to drive home for Christmas, although, I will probably never disclose that to him. He's just really making me feel terrible about it. Honestly, even I can admit to myself that maybe I shouldn't have left Charleston. I just couldn't fathom the idea of spending Christmas there all alone, especially after having to spend Thanksgiving there by myself when I had been expecting my family to come down to spend it with me. Unfortunately, it didn't work out the way we had planned. Then with the restaurant closing and being out of a job, I just really needed to spend some quality time with my family.

I take a deep breath and exhale slowly. Then, I do it again and again to help calm myself down. I have to do something to try to forget about Max and what he thinks of me. I pinch my lips tightly together, irritated with myself for how I'm reacting to him. I don't know why I'm letting his impression of me bother me so much. I usually don't let that kind of thing get to me. I know I can't please everyone no matter how much I try, but for some reason with Max, I just can't push it out of my head, even though I just met the man. I really don't get it.

I attempt to gulp down the lump in my throat and push thoughts of Max out of my head as much as possible. I hesitantly look up at both Judy and Charles, trying to refocus my attention. I force a half smile. Then I reattempt a brief explanation of what happened with my car. "It really was an accident," I maintain. "I just wanted to get home for Christmas," I emphasize. My heart clenches painfully, knowing I still have a long ways to go to make it home to my family. I pinch my lips tightly together in both frustration and defeat.

Judy nods in understanding and offers me a comforting smile. "I know, Dear. Don't worry about him," she insists, giving a nod in the same direction Max just exited. "He's been towing cars all night," she justifies.

Charles nods his head in agreement. Then he emphasizes, "It was a really tough night. He hasn't slept at all."

I force a wider smile and glance back and forth between both of them. They've both been so kind to me. I need to make a concerted effort to show them how much I appreciate their hospitality, especially during this busy time of year. The last thing I want is to cause them to feel bad, just because Max and I don't seem to get along. He is their son. I can only hope that his reason for being so hard on me truly is because he's exhausted. Then again, he wasn't very nice to me earlier tonight when he found me stranded on the side of the road, either. I nod my head and barely look up at them as I mumble, "It's okay. I understand."

Judy steps up next to me and sets a plate filled with food down in front of me. "Sit. Eat," she encourages.

I eye the plate of food and take a deep breath, inhaling the delectable scents from the frittata. I smell sausage, tomatoes, peppers, basil and some other faint spices I can't pick out quite yet. "Wow, that looks delicious," I admire.

Charles nods in agreement as he inhales deeply and grins at me. "Trust me, it is," he confirms. Then he eagerly takes another bite of his own frittata.

I reach for the same stool I was just sitting on and slide it out from the massive black, tan and grey speckled, granite countertop. I admire the large white wooden cabinets underneath the granite as I sit down. In the middle of the island, directly across from the stove sits a deep stainless steel sink. Without Max distracting me, I finally take the time to look around their impeccable kitchen, decorated beautifully for Christmas. The large, open, professional looking kitchen is honestly the kind of kitchen I always dreamed of having one day in my own home. All of the appliances are massive and top of the line. The stove has a large silver hood with six electric burners, so I could have several different things cooking at once. The cabinets up above the stove have thick red ribbons down the front with a large bow, causing them to look like a wrapped Christmas present. The cabinets without the ribbons and bows have clear glass in the middle, so I'm able to see all the dishes stacked neatly inside. A second sink is positioned in the corner on the same wall as the stove. Then just through the doorway, beyond, there is a large bar area and a walk-in pantry; the kind that I've only ever dreamed of. Even the refrigerator blends into the rest of the kitchen, with the doors accented with the same white cabinet wood and moldings on the front of it.

A large red poinsettia in a cherry red painted planter sits on one of the smaller counters to the side, while a tall clear container filled with mini candy canes sits in the corner near the stove. I can't help but notice they even have some Christmas spatulas in both red and green, with snowmen, reindeer, candy canes, or Christmas greetings, placed in a wide-mouth olive green vase right next to the stove for easy access. The Christmas atmosphere in this home and the kindness Judy and Charles are both showing me, definitely helps me feel a little better. I might even say it helps me bring back a little more of my Christmas spirit. Plus as a bonus, it helps me forget about Max. At least that's what I'm going to tell myself right now.

"I love your kitchen," I sincerely express to both of them.

"Thank you," they reply in unison.

I glance back down at my food and pick up my fork. I inhale deeply one more time, a small smile upon my lips. "This really smells great too," I emphasize.

Charles puffs up his chest slightly and nods fondly in Judy's direction. "Judy is the best cook in town," he states, with complete confidence. "She would've had her own restaurant if she didn't become mayor," he adds, proudly. Judy chuckles, blushing slightly.

"Really?" I prompt, instantly curious.

"I don't know about my own restaurant," Judy grins, modestly. She gives a slight shrug of her shoulders, brushing off the compliment.

Charles gives Judy a knowing look and continues to boast about his wife. I smile at him, enjoying the obvious pride he has for her. In the short time I've been here, it's already completely apparent to me how much they love each other. I want to have the same kind of relationship with the man I hope to marry someday, whomever he may be. They actually remind me of my mom and dad too, especially Judy. At least that helps to make me feel more at home if I can't be there. If only Max didn't dislike me so much. "Judy had the plans all drawn up, but she decided to get into politics instead," he enlightens me.

"That's only part of the story," Judy declares, with a teasing glance towards her husband. He arches his eyebrows in question and she looks back at me to further explain. "Charles took over his father's auto body shop about the same time. We decided we couldn't start-up and run two businesses at once," she adds as a reminder.

Charles shrugs and nods his head in agreement. "I guess that's part of it," he acknowledges, remembering.

I can imagine that was a tough decision for both of them, but I admire how it seems they do everything together. They have both already shown me so much of whom they are and the wonderful relationship they share. I can't help but respect both of them greatly for it. Plus, I seem to have a lot in common with Judy. It will definitely give us a lot to talk about while I'm here, especially when it comes to food and dreams it seems. I smile and confess, "I've always wanted to own my own restaurant."

"Really?" she questions, with an arch of her eyebrow.

I nod in confirmation, "Yes. I went to culinary school in Charleston," I happily inform them. "Then, I stared working at a nice restaurant down there as a sous chef. Unfortunately, the place just closed and I've started looking for another job," I add, with a grimace. It's not like working there had been my dream job, but I will miss it. I really enjoyed working in the kitchen, but being able to do that in the kitchen of my own restaurant, with my own recipes one day has always been my ultimate goal. I'll get there some day.

Judy and Charles exchange thoughtful looks. It's almost like they're having a full conversation, without actually saying anything at all. Then again, my parents do the same kind of thing all the time. Sawyer always jokes about it. "Well, isn't that interesting," Charles ponders.

"We have to share some recipes," Judy suggests. She leans up against the counter, moving closer to me.

I happily nod in agreement, knowing I was just thinking the same thing. "Sure, that would be fun," I concur. I love learning new recipes I could try. My mind immediately begins racing to some of the recipes I could share with her that they might enjoy. I have a perfect chili recipe for a cold day like today. Plus, I love baking special Christmas treats this time of year, especially Christmas cakes and cookies. "I mean, it looks like I'm still snowed in," I concede, with a small smile. I gesture towards the windows, where snow still heavily falls outside. "So I may be here a while," I add, grateful to no longer feel quite so alone.

"Speaking of which, I better walk on over to the shop," Charles announces. He wipes his mouth on his napkin and sets it down on his dirty plate. Then he pushes his stool back and stands up. He gathers his dirty dishes and walks around the counter, towards Judy. He holds his dishes out to the side while he tilts his head down to her and she tilts hers up, peering lovingly up at him. He kisses her sweetly, before stepping around her and placing his dirty dishes in the sink. He tosses his dirty napkin in the garbage before he reaches for the sponge to clean his dishes. Judy immediately stops him, with a gentle touch to his forearm.

"Just leave your dishes in the sink. I'll take care of them for you, Charles," she instructs, kindly.

He sets down the sponge and turns back towards his wife. "Thank you, sweetheart," he affirms, his grin never leaving his lips.

She nods in acknowledgement and drops her hand back down to the counter. Then she lovingly prompts, "Stay warm."

Charles nods in acknowledgement and grins at his wife. "I will," he promises, sweetly. He takes a step back and shifts so he's facing both of us, with his back to the kitchen doorway. "I'll see you ladies later," he proclaims. Then he offers us both a small wave before he turns around and strides out of the kitchen.

"Bye, Charles," I call to his retreating back. I return my focus to the plate of food in front of me and finally lift my fork, taking a bite of my breakfast. I can't help the appreciative moan that escapes my lips, as bursts of spicy and savory flavors hit my tongue. "Mm," I mumble, favorably. I chew the food in my mouth and swallow the frittata, before I convey to Judy how much I truly love it. "This really is delicious, Judy," I praise her, enthusiastically. "Thank you!" I declare. I grin and take another bite of my frittata, suddenly starving.

"You're welcome," she replies, smiling gratefully.

I take a sip of my coffee between bites. My mind almost immediately drifts back to thoughts of Max without my consent. I take another bite and focus on chewing, hoping it will stop me from asking his mom any questions about him. I don't want her to get the wrong idea. Then, maybe when he wakes up later, it will be better between us. Maybe he'll have a change of heart when it comes to his opinion of me and it will be like meeting him for the first time. I gulp my food down over the lump in my throat. At least, I'm going to keep hoping that will be the case, unless he proves otherwise.

Chapter 7

Max

I take a deep breath and hold it momentarily, hoping the slightly cooler air in the garage will help me calm down. I exhale slowly and attempt to forget about the woman who's invaded my space, my mind and my home. I heave a sigh and look around at the white wire shelves spread out around the garage. They're all covered with colorful bins and decorations from various holidays throughout the year. My eyes drift back to the large section full of more Christmas decorations and I can't help but wonder if my mom missed those or maybe she'll want me to put some of them up for her today before the Christmas party. I run my hand through my hair and let my hands fall to my lap. I close my eyes and drop my head back against the closed door behind me.

I heave another heavy sigh and my mind drifts back to Ivy. I give my head a shake and begin contemplating why I'm having such a hard time being nice to her. She's absolutely beautiful, but it's almost like I'm acting as if I've never spoken to a beautiful woman before. Plus, she's stuck here with us, whether I like it or not. I'm sure she'd rather be spending Christmas with her family in Boston. Instead of going easy on her when she's probably having a difficult time being so far away from home, all I want to do is push her buttons. I'll even admit I'm acting as if I were back in Kindergarten again, which is ridiculous.

Besides, I don't even know her. I just can't deny that there's something about her that attracts me and makes me pay attention. I guess that's also why I want to push her away as quickly as possible too, before she has a chance to know the real me. I don't want to give her the opportunity to do any damage. Maybe that's why I feel like I can't stop the ridiculous things that come out of my mouth when she's in the room. I don't remember the last time a woman could push my buttons like that and get such a strong reaction out of me, if there ever even was one. I know my mom and dad aren't happy with me for how I'm acting either, which makes this whole situation even worse. I don't blame them. After everything that has happened this past year, the last thing I want to do is fight with my family. They're the most important things in the world to me.

The door opens behind me, instantly startling me. I jump up to my feet as my dad steps out into the garage. He's wearing his dark tan corduroy winter coat, obviously leaving for the auto shop. "Max!" he exclaims, the moment he spots me on the wooden steps. "What are you doing out here?" he questions. Then he pulls the door closed behind him.

I grimace and lean back against the doorframe behind me. I grunt and hesitantly admit, "Cooling off."

He pinches his lips tightly together, obviously disappointed with my response. "I told you to go to sleep," he repeats.

I huff in annoyance and cross my arms over my chest. I remind him, "I'm not a child anymore, Dad."

He arches his eyebrows with doubt, irritating me further. "Then stop acting like one," he demands, nearly echoing my thoughts from only a moment ago.

I exhale slowly, still trying to pull myself together. I know he's right, but I just can't stop the way I feel. I barely make it a few seconds before I blurt out the question that's been sitting on the tip of my tongue since I got home last night to find Ivy staying in our guest room. "What is that girl doing here?" I probe, petulantly.

Ironically, I feel like my irritation has nothing to do with Ivy and everything to do with attempting to let go of everything that's happened this past year.

His eyebrows draw together in disbelief at my question. "She needed a place to stay," he says, stating the obvious.

"So?" I prod, bitterly, feeling like the little kid he just accused me of being. "We're suddenly a hotel?" I add, sarcastically.

Dad shrugs like it's no big deal, causing me to tense even more because it is a big deal to me. In my heart, I know it's not really about Ivy. I don't know anything about her. Although, it would help if I wasn't so attracted to her, but I'm not about to admit that out loud to anyone. I can only imagine what my mom would do if she knew. He replies simply, pulling me out of my thoughts. "You know your mother," he proclaims, in explanation.

I grind my jaw, frustrated because I do know my mother. She's always doing everything she can to help everyone. It's who she is and I love her for it, but sometimes I wish she just concerned herself with us. I know we're always her first priority, but it doesn't always feel that way. I exhale slowly, trying to keep my mouth shut, knowing I'm being selfish, but I just can't stay quiet. I irritably blurt out, "When's it going to be just us, Dad?" I don't remember the last time we spent Christmas just us. After this past year, is it really so wrong to want to spend the holiday with my family, without all the extra people around? I grimace; telling myself my annoyance has nothing to do with the fact that Ivy is such a beautiful woman. Although, having her around to distract me is the last thing I need.

"We have responsibilities," he begins.

I immediately interrupt him, shaking my head in denial. I fervently maintain, "Not to strangers, we don't."

Dad sighs heavily, as if he's exhausted with this conversation, or maybe with me. I'm honestly not exactly sure which, but at the moment, I don't even know if it matters. "Max, it's Christmas," he reminds me, emphatically; even though that's not something I would ever forget. "It's a time to open your heart..." he begins.

I grunt in aggravation and run my hand roughly through my hair. Then, I grumble testily under my breath, "And apparently our home, too."

"That's enough," he firmly demands, leaving no room for argument.

I wince at his reaction, knowing I pushed it too far with my bad attitude. He's the last person I want to stress out. I immediately mumble, "Sorry."

"Look, Ivy isn't going anywhere," he tells me. "For a while, anyway," he adds. "Not with this weather," he stresses.

I sigh and nod my head in understanding. It's not like we have the power to stop the snow. "I know. I know," I relent.

"Make the best of it," he insists, firmly.

I turn to him, my skepticism obvious, but I can't help it. I really thought things would be different this year, especially with this big snowstorm. I thought it was going to be our chance to spend some quality family time together after having such a hard year. I feel like we deserve a break in the right direction. Instead, I'm stuck in my house with a beautiful woman who seems to be on a mission to push all my buttons. "Make the best of having some spoiled princess staying in my home for Christmas?" I question, irrationally.

Dad narrows his eyes at me. "Our home," he emphasizes, firmly, as he gives me another steady look of warning.

I huff in annoyance. "Whatever," I grumble, defiantly. "She's a spoiled brat. She shouldn't be here," I reiterate.

He visibly flinches at my word choice, but thankfully he doesn't scold me again for my comment this time. Probably because he knows I'm not in the right place to actually listen to what he's saying. "But she is, Max," he reiterates, attempting to get through to me. "And maybe she's supposed to be," he suggests.

I arch my eyebrows in surprise and smirk at him. "Now you sound like mom," I announce, teasing him.

He chuckles and nods in agreement. Then, he shrugs his shoulders and concedes, "Thirty years of marriage will do that to you."

My chest clenches painfully just thinking about how we almost lost him. If we had, there wouldn't have been any more years to add to that number. No more birthdays, or celebrations, or Christmases. With those dark thoughts, I clear my throat, believing I have to give one more push. "Dad, please look at her car as soon as you get to the shop," I plead with him, feeling slightly desperate. At least if he's able to get her car fixed, we'll be able to get her on the road to Boston and out of our house that much sooner.

He nods in agreement. "I will," he promises.

"I really want her out of here," I grumble. I know I'm being completely irrational, but that doesn't seem to stop me.

He grimaces again and nods in understanding, "I know."

I sigh, feeling the need to defend myself for my somewhat unreasonable behavior. "It's just, this was supposed to be Christmas just for us this year. This snowstorm," I say and gesture towards outside, "felt like a blessing. It all but guaranteed no one would just drop by," I add, trying to explain the desperation I'm feeling. Our house is the one where the door is always open, especially since mom became the mayor. I bite my lip, hesitantly, but then release it and finally painfully concede, "It was a hard year, Dad."

He huffs a humorless laugh and gives a slight shake of his head. He declares, "You don't have to tell me."

I wince marginally at his reaction, mad at myself for even bringing it up. I grind my teeth and take a deep breath to calm my anxiety. I gulp down the lump in my throat and nod solemnly. "I know," I finally rasp, regretfully.

"It could have been much worse though, Max," he reminds me. He's always able to blow me away with how positive he remains.

I sigh, feeling emotionally exhausted just thinking about it. I take a deep breath and nod again. "Yeah, I know that too," I concede.

He pauses briefly as he carefully assesses me, contemplating our conversation. Then he meets my gaze and announces, "I'll do what I can on the car."

I breathe a sigh of relief, knowing it may not be enough, but that's okay. I offer him a grateful smile, knowing that's all I really need right now. "Thank you," I tell him appreciatively.

"But I'm not sending her out driving in the blizzard," he maintains, giving me his familiar stern look in warning.

"Fair enough," I agree with a small smirk. I wouldn't throw her out in the storm either, even if I might be acting like that's exactly what I would do. I really don't want anything to happen to her. I just want to spend Christmas with only my family for once. I feel like we need this holiday just for us after everything that's happened. Now that things are finally looking better, I want the time to really appreciate being together. I'm just grateful I moved back home when I did to help them. Nothing is more important to me than family. "When's it supposed to stop snowing, anyway?" I question, attempting to change the subject.

"Christmas morning," he reveals.

I groan in annoyance and drop my chin to my chest, feeling completely crushed by the news. "Oh, come on," I complain.

The corners of his mouth twitch up in amusement at my reaction. He firmly repeats, "Go to sleep, Max." He claps his hand on my shoulder and gives me a gentle nudge towards the house. "I'll see you later," he proclaims.

"Fine," I grumble my agreement. "Bye, Dad," I reply, with a tired smile. I wait a moment as my dad walks away. Then I take one more deep breath as I turn and open the door back into the house. I step inside the mudroom full of coats, boots and other outdoor gear and close the door softly behind me. I quietly escape upstairs to my room, finally ready to go to sleep. I may not have said it out loud, but my dad's right. I need to get some sleep and try to make the best out of everything the next couple of days, whether Ivy is still here or not. Hopefully, things will start to turn around for the better again, for Ivy too. We need a quiet family Christmas, where we can just focus on some quality family time, after this tough year.

Chapter 8

Ivy

I slip into the spare bedroom and reach for the phone on the nightstand. I haven't really had the chance to talk to my brother, Sawyer since I've been stuck here and we usually talk nearly every day. I sit on the bed and fold my legs up in front of me, before I dial our home phone number. It still feels strange to have to dial the number, but it's also one of the only numbers I can remember without looking it up in my cell phone. He answers on the first ring, "Hello?"

"Good morning, Sawyer, it's me," I greet him.

"Hi, Ivy," he replies, with a smile in his voice.

"How are you?" I inquire.

He chuckles softly, "I think the question is how are you?"

I sigh heavily and reply, "I'm okay."

"What do you mean you're okay? Are you not comfortable with the people you're staying with or something?" he stammers, anxiously. "We can figure out," he begins.

I quickly interrupt him, before he thinks the worst. "No! No," I insist. "They're very nice." I hear Sawyer's sigh of relief, as Max enters my thoughts and I wrinkle my nose in displeasure. I can't help but add, "I mean, everyone except for Max."

I hear Sawyer take a sip of his coffee, before he questions, "Who is Max?"

I start picking fake lint off the blanket in front of me, needing to do something with my hands. Then, I twist around and pull a pillow into my lap, flipping it around and around, nervously. I finally groan and answer, "Max is the tow truck driver that picked me up last night."

"Okay," he says, drawing out the word as if asking for more. "So what does he have to do with the mayor and her husband?" he prompts, sounding perplexed.

"Max is their son," I swiftly blurt out. Then, I hold my breath and bite my lower lip, anticipating Sawyer's reaction.

"You're kidding!" he exclaims, obviously shocked.

I wince and release my breath slowly. I grumble, "I wish. He keeps calling me princess," I inform him, annoyed just thinking about it.

"He's not far off," Sawyer teases, chuckling into the phone. When I don't respond to his remark, he continues and advises, "Ivy, seriously, just ignore him."

I huff a humorless laugh. "It's kind of hard when there are only four of us in the house and there's not really anywhere else to go," I remind him. "Besides, he's so annoying," I emphasize.

"Ives, you just met the guy. How annoying can he be?" Sawyer prods, attempting to rationalize with me.

"He nags me. He keeps saying that I shouldn't have tried to drive home and beat the storm," I complain.

"He's right, though. You shouldn't have," Sawyer points out, again.

"Sawyer!" I scold. I glare at him through the phone, even though he can't see me. I don't want to hear that from him, whether he's right or not. "You're my twin brother. You're supposed to be on my side," I remind him, as if he doesn't know.

Sawyer bursts out laughing. He doesn't even try to hide his amusement at my reaction. I glare at him again. "All right, all right," he mumbles, placating me as he quiets his laughter. "You'll be out of there soon enough and then you never have to see him again," he reminds me.

I grimace and heave a heavy sigh. "Not soon enough," I grumble.

"Look, he probably sees a lot of accidents. It sounds like he was worried about you," he suggests as an alternative.

"Worried about me?" I ask in disbelief. "He just met me," I reiterate for emphasis.

"True, but..." Sawyer mumbles.

A light knock at the door disrupts my train of thought. "Sawyer, I have to go. I'll call you later," I announce, cutting him off.

"Okay," he agrees. "Bye, Ivy."

"Bye," I reply. I hit end on the call and drop the phone in my lap.

"Come in," I call.

The door swings open and Judy appears, offering me a friendly smile. "Ivy, I'm so sorry to bother you," she begins.

I shake my head, brushing off her apology. "You're not a bother," I insist. "I was just talking to my brother," I explain, gesturing to the phone in my lap. "What's up?" I question.

"The catering company had a pipe burst," Judy grimaces. "They're not going to be able to cook for tonight's party," she explains.

"Oh, that's terrible!" I exclaim. "Can I do anything to help?" I offer. I can imagine how stressed she must feel when all of a sudden she doesn't know how to get all the food prepared for her party tonight.

Judy grins, appearing relieved by my response. "I was hoping you would ask! Do you mind cooking with me?" she proposes, looking hopeful.

I jump up off the bed and stand in front of her, happy to help. "Not at all! This will be fun!" I exclaim, honestly.

Her smile grows even more and her whole body relaxes as she hears the excitement in my reply. "Great," she expresses.

"What do you have in mind?" I ask.

She pinches her lips together, appearing thoughtful. "I don't know," she ponders. "We need to plan everything out," she mumbles, thoughtfully.

"What time is the party?" I inquire.

"It starts at four-thirty and runs until people go home," she informs me.

I nod my head in acknowledgement, as ideas already begin to take root in my mind. "Okay," I reply. "Why don't we do a variety of hot and cold appetizers, a few main dish trays and a dessert buffet?" I propose.

"Cookies and mini-pastries?" Judy questions.

I nod, smiling, "Exactly!"

She grins, "Sounds perfect."

"Do you have some paper?" I prod. For a party like this, I need to write things down to keep myself organized. Plus, we are limited on time, so I want to be sure not to make anything too complicated.

"Of course," she confirms. "Let's plan downstairs, so I can see what I actually have here in the house," she recommends.

"Is the grocery store open?" I probe.

She gives a slight shake of her head, "No, but we can get ingredients we're missing from neighbors. We don't have a lot of time, though."

"Relax," I encourage, hoping I'll help her stay calm. The only thing I can do now is try to help. "This is going to be so much fun!" I exclaim, truthfully. "Let's go plan," I declare.

I stride past Judy, feeling giddy with the excitement of cooking for other people. I walk down the stairs and into the kitchen with her trailing behind me. I take a seat at the same counter where we sat to eat breakfast. She grabs a pad of paper and a pen from one of the drawers before she sits down next to me. "Why don't we talk about a few possible food options and then we can take a look at what I have in my pantry to figure out exactly what we need," she suggests.

"Perfect," I agree.

"Well, maybe we should start out with some basics," she recommends, "like cheese and crackers."

I nod in agreement, "I can make a really good cheese ball and we can add some fruit with that, like red and green grapes for both taste and color."

"Okay," she concurs and begins writing. "That sounds good," she agrees.

"I have a great recipe for a spinach-artichoke dip inside a puff pastry," I offer. I love the idea of a little bit of Christmas green in the foods if we are able to do it.

"Oh, that sounds delicious," she grins.

I nod and inform her, "I can even make it look like a Christmas ornament to make it more festive." I'm getting more and more excited about cooking for her event as we're talking about it. Then again, I honestly can't believe I'm going to help make all this food for the mayor's Christmas party. Plus, she said the whole town is coming. I never thought I would have an opportunity like this so soon after finishing school, even if it is last minute. Although, I may never see any of these people again, it's still a wonderful opportunity for me to do something I love for other people and get a fantastic experience.

"What a great idea!" she exclaims. "And we have to make gingerbread men," she adds, rapidly continuing to take notes.

"And women!" I grin.

"And children!" she smiles.

I glance down at the small, lovable, white dog at my feet. I smirk and playfully add, "And dogs!" The dog barks in agreement, causing both of us to burst out laughing. I catch my breath and inquire, "What kind of dog is she?"

"She's a Havanese. Her name is ColeCole," she enlightens me.

"She's adorable," I praise, with a small smile on my face. I lean down towards the dog and give her a light scratch behind her ears.

"Do you have any pets?" she asks, curiously.

I nod my head in confirmation, "Yes. We have a Pomeranian named Brownie. She's an adorable ball of brown fur," I grin. My heart clenches just thinking about Brownie and home. I want to be with my family for Christmas, but I need to focus on the good things about being here instead. I'm truly overwhelmed at the kindness Judy has shown me. I glance up at her, with an intense need to tell her how I'm feeling. I take a deep breath and gulp over the lump in my throat. I steel myself before I open my mouth. "I know you said to stop thanking you, Judy, but I need to say it again. Thank you for opening your home to me. You don't know how much I appreciate it," I insist. I honestly can't imagine what I would've done if she hadn't offered to bring me home with her last night. Goosebumps cover my body at the possible reality.

She smiles, modestly and attempts to push away the compliment. She declares, "It's nothing." Then she emphasizes, "Really."

"No, it is," I contend. "It really is. I've never had a Christmas away from my parents or brother before," I reveal. "I'm twenty-five years old and this is my first

Christmas without them," I admit, sheepishly. "I always thought that I would be spending my first Christmas away from my family with the man I'm going to marry, but then we would drive over to my parents' house for dinner. Or they would come to our house." I sigh and shake my head at myself the moment I realize I'm rambling about my dreams for my future. I clear my throat and continue, "Regardless, I never pictured spending Christmas without them."

"You're really close to your family," Judy observes.

I nod in confirmation, "I am. My twin brother, Sawyer, is my best friend. We went through everything together, until I moved to Charleston for Culinary school."

"How long have you been living there?" she prods, curious.

I shrug my shoulders and contemplate the answer. "Including school, I've been there for three years," I divulge. "But, like I mentioned before, the restaurant I work at is closing and I don't really have anything else down there. I guess I just wanted to be with my family to recharge, you know?" I explain.

She nods in understanding and confirms, "I do."

"I'm thinking about giving Charleston up and just moving home," I voice out loud, for the first time.

"You aren't happy there?" she prompts.

I sigh and shake my head. "No, not really," I concede. "All of the friends I made during school got jobs in big cities and moved away."

"No boyfriend?" she asks, the corners of her mouth twitching upwards.

I giggle at the question. "Judy, I don't even have a cat," I state, smirking. Judy chuckles at my response. I grimace and shrug, feeling overwhelmed with emotion. I fiddle with a napkin between my fingers, before quietly admitting, "It's lonely there."

"Well, maybe that's the reason you got stuck here," she offers, her eyes sparkling like she's privy to information I don't have.

"What do you mean?" I prompt, perplexed.

"To show you that you belong somewhere else," she grins, thoughtfully. "To show that there are people that you haven't even met yet that are more than willing to open their arms to you and would love to be a part of your life," she elaborates.

I pause, considering her words. I can't help but think, that sounds like something my mom would say. I begin nodding slowly in agreement and tilt my head slightly to the side as I smile over at her. "Maybe you're right," I admit.

"She usually is," Max's deep voice interrupts, causing me to jump in my seat and spread tingles down my spine. I spin around, meeting his gaze. My heart leaps into my throat and I hold back a gasp at the sight of him leaning in the doorway. He's standing casually, with his arms crossed over his chest, causing his biceps to bulge. He appears freshly showered, clean-shaven and he's wearing different clothes. He has on dark blue jeans, a black fitted t-shirt, along with a red, black and gray flannel shirt, hanging open over the top. His green eyes are sparkling and he's actually smiling at me, completely taking my breath away.

Chapter 9

Max

I lean against the doorframe leading into the kitchen, watching Ivy and my mom laughing, chatting and making plans for the Christmas party later today. My stomach twists into knots, the moment I realize Ivy is helping my mom with the food for tonight. I can't help but feel guilty for how I treated her and yet she's here going out of her way to help us. Well, to help my mom, anyway. I gulp down the lump in my throat and reluctantly admit to myself that I'm grateful she's here. I don't know what would happen if it was just me trying to help my mom. No one would want that. It would be a complete disaster.

I suddenly hear Ivy murmur, to my mom, "You're probably right," causing me to smirk in amusement. My mom undoubtedly loves to hear her say that.

I don't even try to stop myself from making a comment. "She usually is," I announce. I smile broadly at Ivy, as I wait for her to turn and acknowledge me. She tenses slightly. Then she slowly twists around and meets my gaze, causing my heartbeat to quicken. I feel my stomach flip-flop from my nerves as I take in her questioning gaze. I honestly do hope she forgives me for the way I've been treating her. I don't want her to feel uncomfortable. My instant reaction was to get as far away from her as possible, but that was just to protect myself and with her staying here, there's no way that's going to happen now. I need to make the best of our situation and part of it is not complaining about spending time with a beautiful woman. It really shouldn't be so tough. I clear my throat, attempting to brush off the anxious feeling in my gut. I swiftly push off the wall, breaking my eye contact with her. "Don't let me interrupt," I tell them both, as I turn away from Ivy.

"You already did," she mumbles. The corners of her mouth twitch up slightly and I realize she's watching me closely for my reaction.

I smile to myself, as I make my way to the cabinet above the coffee pot. I reach up and pull out a white mug with red and green Christmas stockings decorating the outside. I close the door and reach for the full pot of coffee, thankful my mom made a fresh pot. I pour myself some coffee and watch Ivy out of the corner of my eye. She narrows her eyes, glaring at me, as if she's waiting for me to attack, but I guess I can't blame her for that. I notice my mom grinning in amusement, as she looks back and forth between us, while I fight to hide my own smile. I seem to be enjoying my banter with Ivy more and more. Maybe that's why I keep trying to push her buttons. I almost laugh out loud knowing that wasn't the case before, but it could be now. I turn back to face her and then I casually lean against the counter behind me, crossing my feet at my ankles. "Pardon me, Princess," I say, with overt sweetness. I promptly hide my smile with the rim of my coffee cup, awaiting her reaction, but I don't have to wait long.

I notice a spark of anger in her eyes. Her tiny body tenses as her eyes narrow at me. "I told you not to call me that," she reiterates, irritably.

I nod thoughtfully, as if I needed the reminder. I reply, "Right. I'm sorry, Holly," I apologize, knowing that's not her name, but I'm beginning to really like the fire in her eyes when I tease her. I can't seem to help myself, I acknowledge.

"It's Ivy," she reiterates, clearly exasperated with me. She glowers at me, but little does she know, her reaction only encourages me to push her more.

I take a sip of my coffee, attempting to reign in my laughter, before I speak. "Ivy, Holly, they both deck the halls," I chance, with a casual shrug.

"I'd like to deck you," she grumbles. My grin grows and I drop my coffee cup down in front of my chest, no longer hiding my amusement. Her eyes widen in surprise, seeing the huge smile on my face. I anxiously wait to hear what she'll say next.

Unfortunately, I don't get the chance to find out. My mom suddenly steps in between us to garner our attention, as if she's trying to stop two kids from fighting. "All right, you two," she prods, gently scolding us. I chuckle to myself and take another sip of my coffee. I notice the sudden confusion and curiosity in Ivy's expression at the change in my attitude.

My mom immediately attempts to redirect my attention as she focuses on me. "Max," she begins and then waits until I reluctantly turn away from Ivy and pay attention to what she's saying. "We are having the town Christmas party here tonight," she informs me.

I nod in acknowledgement and notify her, "Yeah, Dad told me." It's not like it's a surprise. We all knew she would figure out a way to still have the Christmas party and make sure it's safe to get to. With the party at our house, everyone will just have to shovel the sidewalks and walk here, instead of driving out to the venue in the country.

"Good," she states. "Then, I need you to do something for me," she requests. "I need you to find some ingredients for us."

I nod my head slowly in acknowledgement, as my mom hands me a sheet of lined yellow paper with a list of various groceries she needs to make all the food for the party. I hesitate, remembering the snow, the whole reason Ivy is stranded here and the reason we're having the town Christmas party at our house as well. I wouldn't think anything would be open today. How would people even get to work? I look up at her in confusion and ask, "Is the store even open?" We're one of the few people in town who can get through the streets at all with this much snow, but that's just because we always have our tow trucks ready for any kind of weather, so we can be depended on in situations like Ivy's. We also have a plow attached to the front of all of our trucks this time of year, just in case we need it for something like this.

"No," she answers me, with a shake of her head. "I need you to call the neighbors and see if they have anything on this list or anything else not on the list that they could give us to help with the food for the party. We're still working on it," she adds, referring to herself and Ivy, "but I figured it might take a while to get in touch with everyone and then going to pick everything up," she explains. "So, I thought you should at least get started with collecting ingredients," she clarifies.

I nod in understanding, knowing she's probably right, but I'm not exactly looking forward to it. I sip my coffee, needing the caffeine boost. I quickly skim through the grocery list in my hands, attempting to get an idea of what kind of food I need to try to find for her, but it looks like a little bit of everything from items for appetizers to things for some main dishes and items for baking, the most important in my opinion. "Have you tried calling or texting anyone yet?" I question, hoping she may have at least started the process for me.

My mom shakes her head in response. "No, but you know everyone will try to do something to help if they're able to. Call or text anyone you can think of first, so you don't have to make any wasted trips in this weather," she suggests. I groan inwardly, but remain quiet as she continues. "Unfortunately, if you don't have their number and you can't find it in my book, you'll have to stop by their house and ask them in person. We'll need as much help as we can get," she emphasizes. Without having access to a grocery store or a caterer, that sounds like an extreme understatement. "If they have something they can give us for the party, they can have the first serving," she suggests. "And don't forget to grab some of our recycle bags to carry all of the food in too," she reminds me. "I have a huge stack in the pantry," she adds.

I nod in agreement, willing to do what I can to help. I turn towards the pantry, but suddenly stop to ask her, "Is anybody even home?" I don't really want to walk or even drive all over town fighting all this snow to go to people's houses and ask for help if no one will be home. I don't mind helping, but I don't' need to make it hard on myself either. I was fighting the snow all night. I don't want to do it on my time off if I don't have to.

"Max, you've seen the snow," she reminds me. "I'm sure everyone is snowbound and would love a visitor."

I sigh in defeat and nod in agreement. "Okay, Mom. You're the Mayor," I add, a teasing note in my voice.

She arches her eyebrows and smiles softly at my response. "Thank you, Max," she replies, approvingly.

I nod my head and acknowledge, "And I won't forget to bring the bags with me when I go." I pull my phone out of my back pocket and begin scrolling through my contacts, searching for some of the neighbors' phone numbers.

"Any word on my car?" Ivy inquires, softly, bringing my attention back to her.

I look up and smile at her hopeful expression. I nod in confirmation. "My dad is going to look at it for you today," I update her. "I dropped it off at the shop before I came home this morning," I inform her.

"Thank you," she whispers, appreciatively.

I smile down at her, not able to take my eyes away from her. "You're welcome," I'm finally able to murmur.

"Do you know what's wrong with it?" she asks, curiously. She bites her lower lip, nervous for what I might have to say.

"Besides the two flat tires?" I question. She nods in confirmation. I shake my head in response. "Nope," I answer, popping the p. "I don't look at them. I just pick them up and drop them off," I tell her, honestly.

She arches her eyebrows in surprise. "Real tough job you got there, Max," she responds, sarcastically.

My face falls, feeling as if she just punched me in the stomach. I stare at her in disbelief for another moment, trying to figure out why her comment bothers me so much. She doesn't know me. She doesn't know anything about me. Besides, I've been giving her a hard time, but I can't take it from her? I grimace and give myself a mental shake, tearing my gaze away from hers. I exhale harshly, attempting to let her comment roll off my back, but it's harder than I believe it should be. I reach for my coat, hanging over the back of the chair, knowing I don't want to have to come back in here to get it. I take one last look at Ivy, noticing her slightly apologetic expression, but I don't have it in me to hear it right now. I bite my tongue and turn away from her. I quickly stride out of the kitchen before I say something else to her I don't mean. Some things you just can't take back and I think I might be pretty close to my limit when it comes to Ivy.

I grind my jaw and stalk up to my room, pulling the door closed behind me. I focus on my breathing, attempting to calm myself down. I want to make a few phone calls, before I begin trekking around the neighborhood in search of food for my mom's Christmas party and I want to do it without any distractions.

I pace my room, moving impatiently back and forth from my bed to my desk, slightly on edge, not able to stop thinking about the woman downstairs. I grimace and run my hand through my hair, wondering again why I'm letting her get to me. I've met lots of beautiful women before, but this one seems to push me over some kind of edge I didn't realize I was standing on. Granted, we would have a lot of obstacles to overcome if we wanted to do something about it. Ivy doesn't live anywhere near here. Then, there's the fact that she doesn't even want to give me the time of day, but she's driving me crazy and I'm letting her do it. Then again, I'm obviously doing the same thing to her and I'm enjoying every minute of it. I just don't get my reaction to her. I haven't thought about a woman this much since... My thoughts trail off as my breath catches in my throat. I immediately freeze, as my mind flashes back to tortured memories of my ex-girlfriend. I grit my teeth and exhale harshly, as I attempt to stop the direction my mind wants to go. I have to stop thinking about Ivy. I need to focus on my family and appreciating the time we've been given. I'm ready to make some new family memories this Christmas, especially after this year. A woman is the last thing I need right now. Maybe if I keep repeating it, I'll believe it.

I slowly inhale and then exhale, focusing on my breathing. I need a distraction if I'm going to push her out of my mind. I guess working on this list for my mom will be as good a distraction as any. I force myself to pick up my cell phone and get to work. I go back to scrolling through my contacts, alphabetically. I stop on the first name I see of someone that lives here in Bethlehem, luckily just around the corner. I pull the grocery list out of my pocket and wander over to my desk. I drop down in my chair and set the list down in front of me. I reach for a pen to keep track of where I have to go to pick up the items. Then I tap the name on my phone and try to push Ivy out of my mind, as I wait for Mrs. Anders to answer her phone.

Chapter 10

Ivy

I watch Max walk away, as a sudden wave of guilt washes over me. Pinpricks start in my stomach and claw their way through my chest and up my throat, making me queasy. I didn't mean to make him feel bad, but the hurt look on his face, makes it obvious I did. I just thought with how much he has been teasing me; he could handle me pushing him back a little bit. My heart clenches and I slowly turn back to Judy, nervous for what she might think. I instantly notice the smile on her face and relax marginally, knowing I didn't completely offend her by what I said to her son. At least I don't think I did, I grimace to myself.

"Boy!" she exclaims, bringing my attention to her. "You're really giving it to him," she teases, still smiling.

I feel myself blush and my stomach churns anxiously with her words, but instead of apologizing, I square my shoulders and answer defiantly. "He deserves it. I mean, I know he's your son, but..." I blurt out, defensively. I wince and immediately try to backtrack; afraid I pushed it too far.

Judy grins and cuts me off with a dismissive wave of her hand. She nods and concedes, "Oh, he deserves it." I cautiously exhale a sigh of relief. Then, I laugh along with her, as my body completely relaxes again.

I open my mouth to ask her a question, but then I snap my mouth closed, hesitating slightly. I grimace, knowing my curiosity will get the best of me, telling myself it's because I want to make it better. My tongue peeks out, wetting my lips nervously in anticipation. I just have to ask, "What's his problem, anyway?" After all, he has been really hard on me too and Judy has seen him react that way to me. There has to be a bigger reason he's acting that way, since he seemed so much nicer just now. It's almost like he was a different person. At least, I hope there's a bigger reason.

Judy presses her lips tightly together, briefly forming a thin line, as she gathers her thoughts together. I watch as her face becomes serious, before she takes a deep breath as if steeling herself for what she's about to say. She looks me in the eyes and to my surprise, answers me, honestly. "He had his heart broken," she finally confesses, looking a little bit heartbroken about it as well.

My eyes widen in astonishment and I respond reflexively. "He has a heart?" I probe, sarcastically. She gives me a look I'm very familiar with when it comes to my own mother. It's as if she's disappointed in my question, causing me to immediately regret the words. I wince and I feel my face promptly turn beat red. I nervously clasp my hands together and glance up at her. "Sorry," I mumble, sheepishly.

"He does," Judy declares, pointedly, "but it's behind some pretty thick walls right now," she concedes.

I smile sadly and nod my head in understanding, knowing what it feels like to have my heart broken. "What happened?" I question, curiously.

Judy forces a smile, her eyes defying her, before finally admitting, "It's not easy being the son of the mayor, Ivy."

"Really?" I prompt, surprised. I would think having your mom be the mayor of the town you live in would bring you more perks than anything else. Plus, she seems so nice. "Everyone seems to like you," I insist. Although, I've only met a few people from here, I believe my words to be the truth.

91

"Well, thank you," she smiles, appreciatively. She pauses and takes another deep, calming breath, making me realize whatever she's about to say is really hard for her to talk about. She finally looks back at me and begins speaking again. "Charles got cancer and he didn't really want to tell anyone," she admits. "So, Max quit his job and came home to help us get through it," she explains, simply, almost as if she's telling someone else's story.

My hand reflexively comes to my mouth in shock, as I have a quick intake of breath. My heart clenches tightly at the thought of Charles being so sick. He seems like such a kind man and I hate that he's going through something so tough. I imagine it has to be incredibly hard on all of them. "Gosh, I'm so sorry," I express, sincerely. "I didn't know," I add, regretfully. My heart feels heavier and heavier by the second. Plus, just knowing Max quit his job and came home to help his family causes my whole body to ache. I feel even worse for what I said to him, even though I was only joking. He's going through so much and I have to say something terrible like that? It's like I made a joke of their pain and difficulties. I wince just thinking about it.

Judy shakes her head dismissively. "No, it's fine. He has been in remission for a little over a year now," she proclaims, enlightening me. I exhale a huge sigh of relief, knowing he'll be okay. "Max was working in Manhattan and came home to run the business for him," she continues, surprising me yet again. I'm starting to feel like I misjudged him, a lot. "We really didn't want anyone to have to bear the burden of our family issues, so we kept it between the three of us," she explains. My stomach twists into knots just putting myself in Max's shoes.

I understand keeping things private, but my heart aches for all of them. "That's a lot to handle on your own, Judy," I assert.

Judy nods in agreement, "Yes, I know. And I know everyone in this town would've jumped to help us. It was Charles's decision to keep it quiet. He knew in his heart he was going to win the fight, but he wanted to fight in private. I love him and had to respect that," she declares, with obvious love and admiration for Charles.

My eyebrows draw down sympathetically, imagining what it would've been like for her. I can't help but think of my parents and how they would've wanted to handle it. "Of course you did," I agree, understanding flooding through me. "My mom would've done the same thing," I declare, confidently. Although, I can't imagine what it would've been like for them to live through it, not really.

Then, my thoughts immediately go to Max, causing my heart to clench painfully in my chest, just having a hint of what he's gone through recently. If I were living through something like this with my parents, I would've at least had Sawyer by my side. He would've been there to help me and to talk to when I needed him and I would've done the same thing for him. I can't help but wonder who Max has had supporting him through everything.

"I helped build this town to what it is and I couldn't focus on Charles, the town, the house..." she trails off, the memories taking an obvious toll.

I nod and quietly concede, "It's a lot."

Judy nods slowly in agreement. "It is," she confirms. She sighs and continues, "So Max came back home to help. He ended up dating this girl for quite a while and he fell in love with her. Later, he found out that she was using him to advance her political career, by being connected to me," she informs me. I gasp in shock at the turn of the conversation. My heart clenches even tighter at the thought of Max worrying about his dad, helping his family and having his heart broken by a woman who was trying to manipulate the situation. I can't even imagine. "He was really vulnerable, with his dad being sick," she reveals.

"That's awful!" I exclaim, hurting for him.

She forces a smile and nods in agreement. "I know. He gave everything up to be here for us and he was completely taken advantage of by this girl," she adds, sounding slightly bitter, but who could blame her?

"What happened to her?" I probe, curiously.

"She moved away," she grimaces. "Her family left, too. It was a pretty bad situation," she concedes, sadly.

I pinch my lips tightly together, regretting everything I've said to Max that might've made him feel bad. My stomach twists into knots thinking about someone betraying you like that when you're already dealing with so much. It's already terrible, but doing something awful like that when he already had enough to deal with is uncalled for. I shake my head in near disbelief. "I'm sorry," I apologize, sincerely. "I really didn't mean to hurt his feelings," I insist, my body tingling anxiously from the inside out.

"He's tough, Ivy. You didn't know. But he isn't just a tow truck driver," she adds, with a pointed look, causing my stomach to twist even more with regret. She squares her shoulders and continues proudly, "He's also Ivy League educated and he left one of the best companies in the country to be here for us."

"I had no idea," I murmur, guilt beginning to overwhelm me. I didn't even really mean anything by it.

She nods in understanding, "I know you didn't. Don't worry about it." She pauses and tilts her head to the side as she assesses me. She offers me a small smile and confidently proclaims, "You're good for him."

"Excuse me?" I ask, eyes wide; completely stunned by her statement. I haven't been very nice to him and for her to say something like that; especially after everything she just confessed to me...I just don't understand.

She tilts her head to the side as if she's contemplating what she's about to say next. Then she enlightens me with what she's thinking. "The way you talk to him, I mean. I don't think he knows what to make of you," she claims, with a crooked smile.

I chuckle and respond, "Yeah, I get that a lot."

Judy's eyes widen in surprise and she declares, "I doubt it. Any young man would be happy to date you," she adds, confidently.

I giggle, nervously and give my head a small shake in disbelief. "No thanks," I blurt out, anxiously. "I'm trying to figure out where my life is going. I don't need any distractions," I insist, wanting to move away from this conversation.

Judy laughs and nods her head. "I understand that," she concurs.

"Let's get started, Judy," I suggest, needing a change of subject as quickly as possible. "We haven't looked in the pantry yet. I'm sure you have ingredients for the base of some of these cookies," I indicate.

She nods in confirmation, "That I do." We both stand and walk towards the walk-in pantry. I breathe a silent breath of relief; thankful I was able to change the subject from Max. The more I hear about him, the more I like him and I'm pretty sure he doesn't like me much at all. I need to keep my distance from him.

We easily pull out ingredients to start making some of the Christmas cookies. When we have everything out, Judy turns on some Christmas music, making me smile as the joyful sounds fill the kitchen. "My mom and I always listen to Christmas music, while we bake our Christmas cookies too," I enlighten her.

She grins, "That's a wonderful tradition. Max and Charles like to help, but I think they do more taste-testing than actually helping." We both laugh at the image of them stuffing themselves with Christmas cookies. My mind flashes to memories of my dad and Sawyer doing the exact same thing.

She hands me a Christmas green apron with a red ribbon tied in a bow in the middle of my chest. An adorable family of snowmen adorns the pockets on both of my sides just below my waist. "Thank you," I smile. I slip the green ribbon over my head and begin tying the red and white polka dotted ends around my back into a bow.

She pulls out another apron from the closet. This one is white, with red and green vertical stripes of different thicknesses down it, with a red ribbon pulled through. She places the ribbon over her head and wraps the red ends around her waist, tying it in a bow in the back. "There! Now we're all ready to get to work," she proclaims, with a satisfied grin.

She begins pulling out bowls, spatulas, whisks, measuring cups, measuring spoons, cookie sheets, cooling racks, pans, roasters, trays, platters and any other tools we might need to make all of the food for the party. I reach for the measuring cups and flour and immediately start measuring some out for the first batch of Christmas cookies, with a smile on my face and hum along with the jolly holiday music.

Chapter 11

Max

I walk in the front door and stride towards the kitchen, carrying several bags of food. I was able to gather everything I needed plus much more from all the neighbors. I didn't even need to go very far to find everything. Everyone was extremely willing to pitch in to help. Plus, a lot of people had stocked up in preparation for both the winter storm and for Christmas, which made this scavenger hunt a lot easier than I expected.

As I approach the kitchen, I hear Christmas music playing softly. I can't help but smile at the cheerful sound. I take one step into the kitchen and freeze, my heart leaping into my throat at the sight of Ivy. She's wearing one of my mom's Christmas aprons, wiggling her hips back and forth to the music, as she whips something in a large batter bowl. I grin and step into the room, slowly striding around the counter. I heave the bags up on the opposite side of where both Ivy and my mom are working. "Hi," I say, announcing myself simply. I again have an overwhelming feeling of gratitude towards Ivy. I'm thankful my mom has her here to assist her. And as a bonus, it looks like they're having a lot of fun. I love seeing my mom smile so much.

Ivy stops what she's doing at the sound of my voice and turns a beautiful shade of red. She glances up at me from under her long eyelashes and smiles sweetly, completely taking my breath away. She walks around the counter and approaches me. "Hi, Max. What'd you find?" she inquires.

I gulp over the sudden lump in my throat and mumble, "A lot of stuff." Then, I turn and begin taking things out of the bags as Ivy stands at my side, helping me. She begins organizing things into different piles and mumbling what each item is for, making me smirk. "Sounds like we're going to be eating really well," I murmur.

She pauses and turns to me with a wide grin on her face and her cheeks still slightly pink. "I sure hope so," she admits.

I nod, wanting to give her some encouragement, "Between you and my mom, I'm not at all worried. It will be great," I insist.

She gives me an appreciative look and I grin in response. Suddenly, out of the corner of my eye, I notice my mom standing with her red spatula covered in cake batter, held up in the air, watching us closely with her own secretive smile.

I give a slight shake of my head, attempting to ignore her and easily focus back on Ivy. "So what can I do to help?" I offer.

Her eyes widen in surprise, the corners of her mouth twitching up. "You want to help?" she questions.

I nod and smile down at her. I honestly don't want to go anywhere right now. "That's what I said," I confirm.

Her smile grows, instantly warming my insides. "I could really use some help with chopping the spinach," she informs me.

I walk towards the sink on the other side and wash my hands. "I can do that if you show me how you want it," I agree.

"Sure," she concurs, happily. She grabs the spinach and sets it next to the sink. "Can you grab a cutting board and I'll get the right knife?" she requests. Then she moves over and pulls a knife out of the bamboo block, before she steps up to an open spot at the counter.

I nod and grab the large bamboo cutting board, before I begin rinsing some of the spinach in the sink. I bring the rinsed spinach over to the cutting board and notice Ivy smiling at me. I shrug, nonchalantly. "My mom taught me well," I grin.

"I'm sure she did," she happily concedes. "Here," she says, as she steps up next to me. She easily chops the spinach in one direction, before changing direction to chop it in the other. "Just like that is fine," she instructs.

"You're good at that," I compliment her, admiring how fast she is with the knife. I'd take my fingers off if I tried chopping it that quickly.

She giggles and blushes slightly at the simple praise. "Thank you," she mumbles. She puts the knife down on the cutting board and steps back, allowing me to take over. I'm not as fast as Ivy, but I get the task done and move on to the next.

I help her slice up more veggies and some sausages, before she announces, "We should take a break for dinner."

My head snaps up and my stomach growls in anticipation of eating more of Ivy's food. "Dinner?" I prompt, my mouth already watering.

She grins and offers me a shrug, like it was no big deal. "I just threw some chicken on along with some of the veggies you cut up, so you helped," she informs me.

I chuckle and shake my head, in slight awe of her. "You tricked me," I chuckle. She laughs in response. The three of us walk over to the kitchen table and sit down, the food already set for all of us. "How did I not realize you were doing this?" I mumble.

She giggles, "I guess you were too busy helping."

I shrug and clasp my hands in prayer. I whisper, "Thank you for this food, Amen."

"Max," my mom scolds, as Ivy tries to hide her amusement.

I shrug and remind her, "I'm sorry, Mom, but we can't sit long if we're going to get everything finished in time for the party."

She smirks at my explanation and shakes her head, but allows me to get away with my excuse this time. I take a bite of the chicken and moan in appreciation as it nearly melts in my mouth. "Ivy, this is so good," I rave.

"Thank you. I'm glad you like it," she grins, satisfied. Then, she focuses on her own dinner. The rest of the short meal remains relatively quiet, as we all eat until our plates are clean.

It's not long before we're back to working making more desserts. My favorite part of baking is usually trying to sneak a few treats without anyone noticing, but with Ivy here, I'm not too successful. I reach for a chocolate chip cookie claiming, "They're my favorite." A few minutes later I steal a gingerbread cookie making the same claim, succeeding in making her laugh, again. I like her laugh. "Mm," I moan in appreciation, as I put the cookie into my mouth. "You are so good at this," I praise her honestly, between bites. She just smiles in response and continues working.

The oven beeps and she slips on a red oven mitt and pulls out a tray of Christmas tree brownies. "We need to add powdered sugar to these, to make it look like snow, but we have to let them cool first," she informs me.

"I can handle that," I grin.

"You want to help me decorate some cupcakes while we wait for them to cool?" she proposes. "I already made the frosting and separated it into smaller bowls to make different Christmas colors," she informs me.

"When did you have time to do that?" I ask, confused.

She laughs in answer, her extreme modesty making me like her even more. "So do you want to help me?" she repeats.

"With the frosting? Definitely," I confirm. She hands me some decorating tools, already filled with red, white and green frosting. I immediately get to work, taking my time to try to make it look good. I finish with a small swirl on top, only getting a little bit on myself. I set the tool down and pick up the cupcake. I turn towards Ivy and proudly hold it up for her to see.

She smiles and nods her head in encouragement. "Good job, Max. That looks great," she commends me.

"Thank you," I grin. "Can I see yours?" I request. She arches her eyebrows and timidly pulls one of her cupcakes out from behind her on the counter. My mouth drops open in awe, as I take in the swirls of the cupcake topping. It appears professionally decorated, but then again, I guess it is. "Wow!" I exclaim, making her blush.

We turn back to the cupcakes and finish frosting all of them. Ivy finishes 4 to every one of mine, yet hers all appear flawless. She glances at me and inquires, "Do you want to add the powdered sugar to the Christmas tree brownies?"

"Sure," I agree. I grab the shaker filled with powdered sugar and begin lightly shaking it over the brownies.

Ivy leans over next to me and probes, "How's it going?"

I grin and playfully blow some of the powdered sugar towards her, hoping to hear her tingling laughter again. "It's snowing," I announce. She easily obliges my silent wish, her laughter filling the room and warming my insides.

"I just finished making a chocolate whipped filling for one of my cakes," she tells me. Want to try it?" she offers.

My eyes widen in surprise. I can't help but smile as I nod in agreement, "I'd love to." She holds up a whisk, covered in a thick, chocolate, creamy filling, making my mouth water. Suddenly, her hand pops out and taps my nose with the filling. I burst out laughing, loving that she's joking around with me.

The counter is soon almost completely covered with Christmas trays, platters and bowls, filled with appetizers, main dishes and desserts. My mouth waters just looking at everything, let alone smelling it all. "It smells so good in here," I groan, appreciatively. I close my eyes and inhale deeply enjoying the delicious sweet and savory scents. Ivy giggles and my eyes snap open, immediately focusing on her. I watch, as she continues arranging cookies on one of the platters.

"I'm exhausted," my mom admits. She takes her apron off and hangs it over the back of one of the chairs.

"We got so much done!" Ivy exclaims, happily.

My mom nods in satisfaction, "We did."

I look around the counter admiring all the food. "It looks great," I tell them.

Ivy grins, mischievously. "I imagine it tastes great, too, judging by how many samples you had," she proclaims, with a teasing note to her voice.

I grin back at her and gladly admit, "Guilty as charged." I pat my stomach for emphasis, making Ivy laugh again. I'm really beginning to love that sound.

"I'm going to take a hot bath and get ready for the party," my mom announces. "Charles should be coming home any minute," she informs us.

"I'll fix him a plate for dinner," Ivy offers.

I smile and my mom looks at her appreciatively. "Thank you, Ivy. And thank you for making dinner for us too."

"My pleasure! I'm glad you liked it," she replies.

"That's putting it mildly," my mom laughs. "If anyone should open a restaurant in this town, it's you," she states, confidently.

"Yeah, who knew a princess could cook so well?" I tease her.

She rolls her eyes at me and asks, "Are you going to call me that for the rest of my life?"

"If you're lucky," I blurt out, grinning wide. Realizing what I just said, I wink at her, wondering if we really are a possibility. I watch as her cheeks turn a beautiful shade of pink, warming my insides.

"Behave, you two," my mom encourages; reminding me she's still in the room. She chuckles as she strides out of the kitchen.

I watch as Ivy goes back to cleaning up the kitchen. "Thanks for helping my mom," I tell her, gratefully.

"It was nothing," she claims, shying away from my appreciation.

I smile and step closer to her. I place my hands on her arms and gently turn her to face me. I need her to really understand the sincerity in my words. "Really, Ivy. Thank you," I emphasize. "I haven't seen my mom laugh and smile this much in a long time," I admit.

She offers me a half smile, followed by a soft gasp. "You called me Ivy," she announces, reverently.

I grin and prompt, "Well, that is your name, right?"

She beams back at me, the look shooting straight to my heart. Then she softly murmurs, "Right."

I gently slide my hands down her arms and grasp both of her hands in mine, never breaking her gaze. My whole body instantly heats, especially where we touch. I want to feel her soft lips on mine. My heart rate speeds up as I tilt my head down towards her, wanting the connection with her. Her eyes flutter closed, drawing me closer. I slowly close my own eyes, when we're barely a breath away. My breathing picks up. She's so close. I can almost taste her on my lips. A door slams from the front of the house, startling us apart. Ivy blushes and looks away, instantly looking embarrassed, causing me to grimace, as I catch my breath. That's not the reaction I'm hoping for, not when we almost kiss.

"Hello!" I hear my dad yell from the foyer.

Ivy spins on her heel and rushes towards the front door to greet my dad. I sigh in defeat and trail behind her, hoping she's not just running to get away from me this time. My dad stands by the front door, shaking off the snow and pulling off his boots and coat. "Hi, Mr. Carson!" Ivy greets him, overly cheerful.

"Hey, Dad," I say.

He turns to Ivy and reminds her, "Please, call me Charles." She nods her head in acknowledgement.

"Everything okay down at the shop?" I inquire.

He nods, "Yeah, but there was a pretty bad wreck down on 87. They were calling for extra tows," he informs me.

"Need me to go?" I ask.

"I don't want to impose on you, especially since tonight is the Christmas party," he replies.

"Dad, it's fine. I'll call in," I offer. It would probably do me some good to step away from Ivy for a few minutes, so I can think straight.

He smiles, gratefully, "Thanks, Max."

I grab my coat and walk towards the mudroom for my work boots. "Will you be back in time for the party?" Ivy questions.

I smile down at her, hoping that means I'd be missed. "You better believe it. I need to work up an appetite!" I proclaim.

She grins, helping to release the tension in my shoulders. She murmurs, "Be careful."

I notice the arch in my dad's eyebrows as he looks back and forth between the two of us in surprise. His reaction spurs me on to make my own escape. "See you guys later," I tell them both and immediately exit into the mudroom.

I slip on my shoes just as I hear Ivy ask, "What?" I chuckle to myself, imagining the look he must have given her for her to ask that.

"That was a change," he observes. "When I left this morning, it seemed like you two were going to rip each other's heads off."

I freeze, afraid to move a muscle, hoping to hear Ivy's response. "Well, 'tis the season of forgiveness. Right?" she suggests, cheerfully.

"I guess so," my dad responds, sounding confused.

"Come on, I'll fix you a plate," she offers, successfully changing the subject.

I smile to myself as I listen to their fading footsteps. I finish tying my work boots before I reach for my cell phone. I want to see if I can find out what I'll be walking into. Plus, I should let them know I'm coming. I finish the call and hang up the phone. Then I walk back into the kitchen to find my dad eating by himself. "Hey, Dad. Where's Ivy?" I question.

"She's calling her family, then getting ready for the Christmas party," he informs me.

"Okay. It sounds like I'm going to be pretty late," I acknowledge. "Seven cars need to be towed," I confirm.

"That many?" he prompts.

I nod in confirmation, "Yeah. A tractor-trailer jack-knifed and took them all out."

"Anyone hurt?" he probes, his eyes wide and full of concern.

I pinch my lips tightly together and shrug, not yet knowing the whole story. "I don't know. Eighty-seven is completely shut down in both directions, though," I enlighten him.

"You don't have to go, Max," my dad repeats.

I sigh, thinking about the chaos I'm about to walk into and the effects it will have on all the families involved, especially this time of year. "I know, but they really need help. If I'm there, it will definitely help move things faster," I answer.

He nods in agreement. "True," he murmurs. He pauses and then looks at me out of the corners of his eyes before he murmurs, "So, Ivy..."

"Don't start, Dad," I immediately interrupt, attempting to stop this conversation before it begins.

"Start what?" he asks, innocently. "It's merely an observation," he comments, trailing off.

"Yeah, I know what you're thinking. It's nothing. Don't put any thoughts into it," I argue.

"Into what?" he mumbles, as if he doesn't know what I'm talking about.

"You know what, Pops," I insist. "Mom was staring at us all day, with that look in her eyes. There's nothing there," I announce, a little bit too defensive.

"I never said there was," he replies, smirking.

"She's still a princess," I argue, weakly.

"Okay, Max," he responds, placating me.

"I mean, it's fine if she stays here for Christmas," I add, remembering our discussion in the garage this morning.

"Oh?" my dad prods, arching his eyebrows in question.

"Well, yeah," I stammer. "She helped mom out with all of the cooking for the party. It would've been way too much for mom to do all by herself."

My dad looks at me, suddenly confused. "Why are they cooking, anyway?" he inquires. "I thought your mom hired Water Lily Caterers."

I nod my head and tell him what mom had told me, "Apparently a pipe burst at the catering hall and they couldn't cook for it."

His eyebrows draw further down in confusion. "Really?" he ponders. "I saw Lily's husband at the shop earlier and he didn't mention that," he apprises me, slightly perplexed.

I pause, finding that strange as well. "Really? That's weird," I mumble.

He nods and continues, "Yeah. He said that mom cancelled the order because of the weather."

"The weather?" I repeat. "That doesn't make sense," I state.

"Yeah, that's what he said," he insists. "Lily was glad not to have to bring all the food over in the blizzard, but..." he trails off, as understanding suddenly dawns on both of us. "Oh," he mumbles, dragging out the word.

"Mom," I grumble. "Really?" I ask in exasperation.

My dad opens his mouth to say something. Then he snaps it closed and shrugs instead.

I sigh in annoyance and shake my head. "I'm out. See you later, Pops," I grumble and turn to leave.

"Max!" dad calls after me, to get my attention.

I turn back towards him, before I prompt, "Yeah?"

"We did not have this conversation," he claims.

I nod in understanding, knowing my mom would probably deny it anyway. Plus, I don't want to hurt Ivy.

107

She was so happy to be able to do something to really help my mom. I sigh in resignation and mumble, "Whatever, Dad." I turn to leave to do what I can to help at the accident. I can deal with all of this when I get home.

Chapter 12

Ivy

I lift my suitcase up onto the bed and flip it open as thoughts of Max continue to completely consume my energy and attention. Since I met him, my feelings for him have been all over the place. He's gone from being my hero for saving me because I was stranded on the side of the road during the middle of a historic snowstorm, to being rude, to taking care of my car for me, to being rude, to being kind, funny and helpful. I really had so much fun with him today. Now I'm overwhelmed thinking about everything he's gone through with his dad this past year and on top of that, finding out his ex-girlfriend just dated him to get ahead. Knowing all of that, I don't blame him for being leery of women, especially someone he just met. Maybe that explains why he has been all over the place with what he says and what he does when it comes to me. He's definitely not looking at me like he hates me anymore. My heart skips a beat. I can admit to myself, that makes me really happy.

I smile broadly as I think about how much fun we had together in the kitchen today. Sounds kind of strange thinking it, but working with him in the kitchen to get all the food ready for the party feels like a blessing. Granted, his mom was obviously a lot more help than him, I think, giggling to myself. But he sure tried and I really enjoyed being able to show him how to do a few things that I know I'm good at. Plus, I feel like we got a chance to talk and learn some of the little things about each other, like favorite foods and the kinds of music we both listen to. I guess it's kind of like the types of things you talk about on a first date. I instantly feel myself blush at the thought.

But if it were a first date, his mom wouldn't have been invited. I chuckle to myself.

I sigh reverently, remembering the way his green eyes looked at me throughout the day. Then after his mom went upstairs to get ready and it was just the two of us, the way he looked at me made my heart race. Goosebumps spread like wildfire all over my skin, as I think about the way I felt being so close to him, barely a breath away. Only to be startled apart when his dad came home. I can't believe we almost kissed. It doesn't feel real. My heart skips a beat at just the thought of kissing him. I can't help but wish his dad would've waited to walk in the door, even just a few minutes later and things might've been a little different. Maybe I wouldn't be questioning myself so much. And maybe I wouldn't be wondering what it would be like to kiss Max, either. I feel my cheeks warm again and my heartbeat quicken as my thoughts run rampant.

The house phone rings, startling me. The shrill sound disrupts my thoughts and I give myself a slight shake, attempting to redirect my focus on the clothes in my suitcase. I need to go through my dresses and pick out something to wear to the party. I do want to look good tonight, for myself. I shake my head, laughing at myself. "Who am I trying to fool?" I murmur. I always like to look good, but I really want to look fantastic for Max. I want to see that adoring look in his eyes again.

I hear the echo of footsteps on the wood floor approaching my room. There's a light knock just before Judy calls my name from the other side of the door. "Ivy," she prompts.

"Coming," I reply.

I turn around and leap towards the door with the adrenaline of my time with Max, still pumping through my veins. I pull the door open to find Judy smiling at me. "Sorry to bother you," she begins, sweetly.

"You're not bothering me," I insist. She's welcomed me into her home. If she needs me for something, all she has to do is ask.

She holds a black wireless house phone in her hand and holds it out towards me. "Your brother is on the phone for you," she informs me.

I grin, excited to talk to Sawyer. "Thank you," I respond, gratefully. I take the phone, thankful for the distraction, no matter how brief it might be. It's not like I've been able to focus on anything except Max anyway.

"I'll give you some privacy," she offers. She gives me a quick wave as she quietly pulls the door closed behind her.

"Thank you," I repeat. I'd been waiting for him to call. I put the phone to my ear as I walk back over to the bed. I climb up and lay on my stomach, propping my head up with my hand under my chin. "Hi, Sawyer," I address him, cheerfully.

"Hey, Ives," he greets me. "You hung up with Mom and Dad before I got a chance to talk to you," he scolds.

"I know, but Mom said you were making cookies. Besides, I knew you would call me back when you had a few minutes to talk," I claim, laughing.

"Oh really?" he questions, as if he's not sure if he should believe me. "I was actually just talking with mom and dad about you," he taunts.

"You were, huh?" I grin, imagining all of them on our worn tan living room couches, gossiping about me.

"Yup," he answers, popping the p.

"You must be really bored without me there if you're spending all your time talking about me," I tease. "Or maybe I'm just that special," I emphasize.

He laughs, but doesn't make another comment, causing me to believe he really does miss me. I smile to myself, but don't call him on it. He enlightens me, "Anyway, they told me you've been pretty busy working today." He pauses, waiting for some kind of response from me. When I remain quiet, he curiously urges, "How did that happen?"

I nod, even though he can't see me. "Yeah," I admit. "I guess the catering company that was supposed to do all the food for the Bethlehem Christmas party had a pipe burst and so they couldn't do it at the last minute. So, when the mayor found out that I'm a chef, she asked if I would be willing to help. Of course I said yes," I apprise him, my excitement apparent. "So, I've been helping cook all day for the mayor's Christmas party tonight with both her and Max," I reveal. "The whole town was invited!" I add.

"Really?" he asks.

"Yeah," I confirm. While I'm talking I push myself up and stand over my suitcase, going back to looking through my clothes to find my dresses and try to decide which one I want to wear for the party tonight. "It was really fun. I haven't had this much fun cooking in a long time," I divulge. I smile thinking about helping Max with the cupcakes. When we started frosting and decorating them, he tried so hard to do it well, but he couldn't figure out how mine looked so different than his. He was so adorable. "Judy and Max were really great," I emphasize, as I start to daydream about Max.

"W-wait," he stammers, as if taken by surprise. "Did you say, Max?" he questions, his tone full of disbelief. "Don't tell me you softened up," he teases me.

I grin as I feel my face heat in embarrassment almost instantly. I know better than to prejudge anyone, but Max knew how to push me just the right amount.

Between his good looks and the way he questioned me about what happened, I just couldn't help but assume the worst. Besides, he was already incredibly rude to me when he didn't even know me. Isn't that the same thing? I question silently. Sawyer would roll his eyes at that kind of response though, so I stammer trying to come up with an answer he won't give me a hard time for, while I pick imaginary lint off my pants. "Well," I begin hesitantly, "There was a lot I didn't know about him," I finally concede, attempting to downplay my initial reaction.

"What?" he gasps, in mock surprise. "Ivy Anderson made a snap judgment about someone?" he probes, sarcastically.

I grimace and retort, "Very funny." I take a deep breath and defend myself, trying to sound casual. "I'm just saying that he might not be as bad as I thought he was," I relent. I pull out three dresses, one red, one green and the third one white and silver with a touch of gold. I have to admit I'm thankful I packed a few options to bring home with me for the holidays. Otherwise, I wouldn't have anything to wear to the Christmas party tonight. I reach up and hang all of them on the back of the closet door. Then I continue to assess them as I talk to my brother.

"Well, you be careful," Sawyer warns, in his big brother tone. I roll my eyes and then smile to myself. I'm grateful he's my brother, but telling him that would only increase his teasing. Ironically, him joking with me more would only make me more homesick for my brother. "Try to enjoy the party, okay?" he encourages.

"I will," I promise. "Love you," I add, sweetly.

"Love you too, Ives," he whispers. "Bye," he says.

"Bye, Sawyer," I return. I immediately end the call and drop the phone down on the bed next to my suitcase.

I stand in front of all three dresses, carefully assessing them, trying to make a decision. The red dress is a cocktail length dress, with a deep V at the neck and a smaller V at the waist. Although it's cute, I don't think it's right for the party tonight. I grab the red one and slip it back into my suitcase before focusing on the next one. I look at the Christmas green dress, admiring it. I love the lacy pattern over the bodice, but I still think it might be too short for tonight. I grab the green dress and quickly put it away. I want to be able to consider the last dress without the other dresses distracting it. I take in the long, silver dress with a white, lacy overlay full of simple daisies. It has light gold accents and a one-inch wide, silky, silver ribbon at the waist. It has a high scoop neck and about one and a half inch thick shoulder straps. I think this dress will be perfect. I love the way the simple A-line skirt flares out slightly. Besides, I wouldn't be surprised if there were a lot of people wearing both red and green tonight. It is Christmas. With this dress I'll stand out, hopefully to Max too. I smile to myself, completely satisfied with my choice for tonight.

"Shoes!" I exclaim, suddenly. How could I have forgotten shoes? I immediately know what shoes will be perfect. I grimace, hoping I remembered to pack the shoes I'm looking for. My silver, strappy two-inch heels will add just the right touch. I pinch my lips tightly together, hoping I find them. I frantically dig through my suitcase. I finally find them on the bottom and breathe a sigh of relief. "Here they are," I announce to myself. I pull them out and set them on the floor near my dress for one last look. I smile to myself, happy with my decision.

I head to the bathroom, ready to jump in the shower and pull myself together. I quickly shower and dry my hair, before I begin putting on my make-up. When I'm finished, I look in the mirror, trying to decide how I want to style my hair. I warm up my curling iron and allow my thoughts to drift back to Max. I wonder if he dresses up for something like this. I would love to see him wearing a tie, but I imagine it's not something he does very often. Hopefully it's not too bad at the accident site. Of course I hope the people are all okay, but I would also like him to be able to make it home to enjoy the party with me.

It's not long before I'm standing in front of the full-length mirror on the back of the door, taking in my appearance. I smile to myself, satisfied with how the dress fits me. I take one more look at my make-up and then I add a touch of red lipstick for a little bit of Christmas color. I decide to pull my hair partially up, leaving the back of it falling down over my shoulders. I grab the hot curling iron and add a few flowing curls to the back, hoping it will give my hair a little more volume. I quickly spray my hair to keep it loosely in place. Then I take a deep breath and exhale slowly as I take one last look at myself in the mirror.

I smile uncertainly at my reflection. It's strange to me that I know my nerves don't have anything to do with the party or with the food we made today. I'm proud of everything I made and I'm confident it will go over well. If I'm being completely honest with myself, my anxiety is due to the anticipation of seeing Max again. I can't help, but hope he likes what he sees when he looks at me. I make a face at myself in the mirror and shrug, like it's no big deal. I remind myself, I'm worth it. If he doesn't think I look good, that's his loss. I didn't even know him a couple days ago. I definitely don't need his approval, just my own.

"I will focus on meeting new people and helping Judy with the food, not on Max," I repeat to myself for what feels like the hundredth time. I close my eyes and take one more deep calming breath and exhale slowly. I open my eyes and push my shoulders back feigning confidence. Then I spin around, feeling my dress swish around my legs, as I stride out of the guest room and towards the stairs, ready to join the Christmas party.

Chapter 13

Ivy

I walk downstairs, barely able to contain my excitement along with the nervous energy building up inside of me. My hand bounces between the garland and white lights wrapped around the railing with each step. I look around, surprised at how many people are already here. The house is filled with people of all ages, dressed up for the occasion in fancy dresses and suits, skirts and nice shirts, sweaters and blazers. I knew Judy was expecting a lot of people, but I almost didn't believe so many would be able to make it here in this weather. "How did everyone get here with all the snow?" I mumble to myself.

"A bunch of us pitched in and shoveled the sidewalks clear, so we could all walk here," an older gentleman with white hair informs me, obviously overhearing me talk to myself. I blush; moderately embarrassed he caught my murmuring. "No one wants to miss the Bethlehem annual Christmas party. We look forward to it every year," he announces, grinning.

I smile up at him, pushing away my awkwardness, as I descend the last step. "And you shouldn't have to. I'm Ivy," I proclaim, introducing myself.

"Ah, yes, Ivy," he grins. He reaches for my hand and places a kiss on the back of it, before releasing it. "I'm Tom," he replies, introducing himself. "My wife, Jenny and I already heard all about you," he informs me, a broad smile lighting up his face.

"Really?" I ask, perplexed.

He nods and leans closer to me as if he's about to tell me a secret. "Don't worry, all good things," he confirms.

I smile politely as I feel my cheeks warm, turning a light pink. "Well, It's nice meeting you, Tom. You'll have to introduce me to your wife later," I request.

"Of course. We'll be sure to come find you later," he suggests. "Right now she's sampling all of the delicious food on the table," he adds with a grin.

I offer him a pleased smile and tell him, "I hope you and your wife have fun." I give him a small wave and spin on my heel, quickly striding towards the kitchen. I want to make sure to help Judy with some of the food trays.

I spot Santa in the middle of a group of kids. I wave at him on my way, knowing its George from the Bethlehem Inn under that white beard. He smiles and calls out, "Ho, ho, ho, Ivy!" Then he turns and smiles back down at the children crowding around him.

I step into the kitchen and pick up a red Christmas platter filled with some of the appetizers we made earlier. I walk into the family room with the tray in hand and immediately approach an older woman with short gray hair, talking to a younger woman with the same warm brown eyes. I smile as they sit down on the curved long black couch, decorated with white Christmas bears wearing red and green sweaters, sitting in each corner. The coffee table in front of the couch has a mirrored top, making the room appear even bigger than it is. A stuffed snowman sits on top of the table with long legs dangling off the side. A tree made up of different colored ball Christmas ornaments sits in the middle, with a red ribbon tied in a bow on top and the ends of the ribbon draped down the sides. A green Christmas tray painted with snowman is displayed there, holding two Christmas candles, next to a nearly empty red tray with appetizers. I hold the appetizer tray out to the two women and offer some to both of them. "Would either of you like to try a sausage roll?" I offer.

The older woman looks up at me and grins. "Why, thank you, Dear," she replies, kindly. She reaches for a small one as I hand both of the women a napkin.

Then, the other woman reaches in and grabs one as well, before glancing at me and mumbling, "Merry Christmas."

"Merry Christmas," I reply. Then I turn towards the fireplace designed with gray, black, and silver, long, thin tiles. I immediately notice the two silver French horns placed a little off to the side of the middle of the mantel because they're similar to the ones on the nightstands in the room I'm staying in. The fireplace is also dressed with white Christmas candles on each end of the mantel. Silver beads swoop down in front of the ledge, until they meet in the middle near a mini Christmas tree, which is only about a foot tall. It's decorated simply with miniature gold and silver ornaments.

To the right of the fireplace, sits a gorgeous Christmas tree, about eight feet tall. It's decorated with white lights as well as a white star on top, shining brightly. The ornaments are all silver and gold, snowflakes, pinecones, Christmas trees, stockings, Christmas balls, bells and other similar items that have always reminded me of the holidays. The tree has accents of beautiful red velvet bows scattered all around. It's so different from how we decorate our tree, but its unique look is one of the reasons I love it so much.

Every year my family decorates our tree with ornaments we've collected throughout the years, from places we have gone or things that remind us of one another. I love how every Christmas tree shows a little bit of someone's personality, making every tree perfect in it's own way.

I turn around and slowly make my way back into the dining room, offering appetizers to guests as I go. A woman about the same age as me stops me and introduces herself to me, "Hi, I'm June. You must be Ivy," she grins.

I smile politely and nod my head in confirmation, "Yes, I am. It's so nice to meet you June. Merry Christmas," I add.

"Merry Christmas," she proclaims. "I was told you made a lot of this wonderful food we're having tonight," she informs me. "Everything is absolutely delicious," she raves.

I blush and mumble my appreciation, "Thank you."

"I'm currently planning my best friend's bridal shower for February. Do you happen to cater parties?" she questions, looking hopeful.

My heart skips a beat at her request. It's a huge compliment to me. "Wow," I murmur. "I'm so sorry, but I'm not from around here," I reveal, regretfully. I wish I were because that sounds like something I would truly enjoy doing.

"Oh, that's too bad," she mumbles, with a frown. "Well, if anything changes, ask Judy for my number," she instructs.

I nod in agreement, "I will, thank you."

"It's nice to meet you Ivy and thank you," she adds, as she turns away.

"Thank you," I call out, again. I continue offering appetizers to guests as I admire more of the decorations. There's vases over two feet tall filled with colorful ball Christmas ornaments, a smaller version of a Christmas tree made up of similar round ball ornaments sitting on the end table in the living room, as well as colorful nutcrackers in different shapes, colors and sizes on various tables as well as in the windows. Christmas candles are scattered all around and even some of the petite, glass appetizer plates are covered with snowmen and Christmas trees. I take a deep breath and the scent of pine trees, and delicious holiday foods fills the air. I smile gleefully, enjoying the feeling of Christmas all around me, even though I'm not at home.

A kind woman with long, black hair, deep brown eyes, and a beautiful lacy, cranberry red top, interrupts my perusing of the decorations. "Oh, I tried some of these," she informs me. "These are absolutely delicious," she praises as she grabs another appetizer off the platter I'm holding. I smile in response, loving how much everyone seems to be enjoying the food. "Thank you," she murmurs, before she walks away.

Judy steps up to me from behind and taps me lightly on the shoulder. She looks stunning, as always, in a Christmas green, button down, silk blouse and silky, black dress pants, with a high waist. "Ivy, Sweetheart," she says, stopping me with a hand to my forearm. "Enjoy the party," she encourages.

"I am!" I declare.

"You don't have to offer food to the guests," she insists, firmly. "You're my guest," she emphasizes.

"I know, but I really am having a good time, Judy. I love seeing how people react to my food," I reveal, honestly.

She smiles, understanding filling her eyes. She eyes the tray I'm still holding and points to the dates on one end. "What are these?" she prods, curiously.

"Max brought back dates instead of apricots, so I made almond-stuffed dates, wrapped in bacon. Want one?" I offer.

"Don't mind if I do," she grins. She picks one off the tray and pops it into her mouth. She chews as I anxiously await her response.

"Well?" I prompt.

She politely covers her mouth with her hand, still chewing. "Amazing!" she mumbles around the food in her mouth.

I grin, completely satisfied. "See?," I prod, holding my hand out towards her. "That's what I love about Christmastime. This is the first time in years that I won't be cooking Christmas Eve dinner for my family," I admit. I love cooking for my family for Christmas and watching them all enjoy my food. "Even when I was little, I used to help my mom in the kitchen, as soon as she'd let me, anyway. I've always enjoyed it," I murmur.

Judy swallows the date and takes a sip of her wine. "Ivy, if it means that much to you, you're welcome to cook for us," she offers, only half teasing.

We both laugh, but I respond honestly, "Maybe I will."

"I'm sure Charles and Max would both love it!" she claims, sounding happy with the idea. "I can be your sous chef," she proposes, with a smile.

"Deal!" I exclaim, excitedly.

Judy pauses and looks around the room, as if she's searching for something or someone. "Speaking of Max, where is he?" she inquires.

My stomach flutters nervously, wondering if he'll make it back soon. "He hasn't come back from the accident scene, yet," I inform her.

She grimaces, faintly. "It's getting late. If he doesn't get here soon, he'll miss all the food," she murmurs, concerned.

I lean in towards her, attempting to keep what I'm about to say between us. "Don't worry. I made him a plate and hid it in the kitchen," I divulge, hoping no one finds it before he gets home.

Judy smiles and pats me lightly on the shoulder in appreciation. "That was very kind of you, Ivy," she proclaims.

I shrug, feeling a rush of color flow into my cheeks at her praise, but I'm not quite sure if it's because of the compliment or because of the way I'm starting to feel when Max is around, or even when he crashes into my thoughts. "Tis the season, right?" I urge, attempting to shrug off the accolades.

Judy nods, giving me a knowing smile and confirms, "Indeed."

The corners of my mouth curve upwards, as I walk away with the tray. I offer appetizers to a few more guests, before I set it down behind Judy on the dining room table, covered with an embroidered, dark Christmas red tablecloth and filled with various decorative Christmas platters, bowls, and trays all full of food. I begin rearranging some of the food and trays under the silver and crystal chandelier, decorated with red velvet bows, to make room for more food. After I'm completely satisfied, I'm left with two empty platters. I take one last look at the table to see if there's something specific I should bring out from the kitchen to replace what's missing.

While I'm leaning over the table, Charles steps up next to his wife and smiles. I give him a small wave, but he's completely focused on Judy and doesn't notice me. I pick up the two empty platters, but before I walk away, I can't help, but overhear them talking. "You know, I think you may have given Max the greatest Christmas gift of all," he murmurs to her.

"Oh, and what's that?" she questions, innocently.

Charles chuckles softly and smiles down at her. Then he whispers, admiringly, "You sure are something, Judy Carson." I turn just as he kisses her sweetly. I grin at how handsome he looks in his black suit, white shirt and red Christmas tie. They are such a beautiful couple inside and out. They remind me of my parents in a way. They have the kind of relationship I hope to have one day with my future husband; whoever that may be. I feel myself blush deeply, as an image of Max in a black tuxedo pops into my head.

I bite my lower lip and give myself a little mental shake to pull myself out of my daydream. Then, I take a deep breath as I spin around and slip away from the table. I move around two ten-year-old boys, with their dress shirts already un-tucked, followed by a little girl in a dark green velvet dress, arguing about which dessert they like best. I smile and nod at the guests as I stride into the kitchen and set down the empty trays next to the sink.

My thoughts start to wander as I put more trays of food together, wondering what Max might be getting for Christmas from his mom and dad. It sounds like they have something really special planned for him this year. I'm happy for him. He deserves it. My heart clenches, strongly believing they all deserve a special Christmas this year. Hopefully, having me here won't interfere with whatever they have planned. I give myself another small shake and remind myself that it's none of my business. I'll just have to make sure to give them some space, so they can enjoy their family Christmas together. I can't help but think, that's only if I'm still here on Christmas morning and my heart lurches in protest, while I keep myself busy, trying to ignore it.

Chapter 14

Max

I walk into my house, filled with family, friends and neighbors, grateful to be home. I weave through the people, giving everyone a smile, a hello nod, and wishing him or her, "Merry Christmas," as I walk by. I'm only stopped a few times and attempt to quickly excuse myself as I head to the kitchen. I'm so hungry. I need something to eat before I can even think about joining the party. I realize there's food in the dining room, but I'm too impatient to wait in any kind of line to find out most everything is gone. Plus, I don't want to be rude and push my way up front or appear anti-social, when food is almost the only thing I'm thinking about at the moment.

I step into the kitchen doorway and freeze at the sight in front of me. Ivy has a cherry red silicone hot pad on and she's pulling cookies out of the oven wearing a gorgeous silvery dress with her hair flowing down her back in soft curls. She looks absolutely stunning, completely taking my breath away. I watch her as she transfers the warm cookies to a tray and places them on the counter before turning back to the oven to retrieve more desserts.

Two pretty, young teen girls walk into the room, both with blonde hair and about the same height as Ivy. One girl is wearing a red dress with a red floral lacy overlay, and an ivory sweater over her shoulders. She has her hair pulled up in a high ponytail, with long blonde curls hanging down her back. The second has a black, white and gray knit sweater dress, with her loose curls falling over her shoulders. Their eyes widen at the site of a full plate of treats, but I don't blame them. They take a step closer and reach out to grab one, when Ivy spins around, noticing them. She steps quickly towards them and gently swats their hands away with her spatula, causing me to laugh quietly. "No, you can't have that!" she scolds, abruptly stopping them in their tracks. Their eyes widen in surprise. "That's for the mayor's son," she announces, causing my smile to grow. She reaches for two chocolate covered marshmallows on sticks, sprinkled with red and green and hands them each one of those with an apologetic smile. "Here, try these," she encourages.

I step further into the room as the girls laugh and quickly leave the room with their treats. "Did I hear you have something for the mayor's son?" I prompt, grinning broadly.

She spins on her heel and meets my gaze. She smiles up at me, causing my heart to skip a beat. "Max!" she exclaims. "You're back!" she proclaims. She sounds relieved, making me happy.

I nod my head in confirmation, "Yeah." I huff a laugh before I admit, "And I'm starving."

"Here, try these," she offers. She reaches for the plate of food she just rushed the two girls away from and happily hands it to me.

I immediately dive in. I pop something into my mouth, not caring what it is. If Ivy made it, I know it will be delicious. "Mm," I groan in satisfaction as I chew a bite. "This is incredible," I murmur.

She smiles, satisfied. "Thank you," she mumbles.

"Really, Princess," I emphasize. "You sure know how to cook," I insist. Then, I drop something else into my mouth.

"Thanks," she replies, giddily, as she beams proudly up at me. "I'm glad you like it," she admits.

"My mom wanted to open a restaurant a long time ago, but my dad started the auto body shop instead," I reveal.

"I know. She told me," she concurs.

I shake my head in awe, as I take a delicious bite of something else that looks to be some kind of meatball. "Man, maybe you can get her to retire from office and start a restaurant with you," I encourage her. That restaurant would have really good food. In fact, that's the kind of place I wouldn't mind going to all the time.

Ivy laughs, but doesn't comment. Instead, with her blue eyes sparkling, she informs me, "Your mom roped me into making Christmas Eve dinner tomorrow."

"Bless her," I mumble my appreciation. I'm already looking forward to it.

"Are you okay with that?" she questions, hesitantly.

I arch my eyebrows, as if to ask if she's joking. When she doesn't say anything else, I vehemently declare, "If it tastes anything like this, absolutely."

She smiles softly and repeats, "Seriously, Max. Are you okay with me being here for Christmas Eve? I feel like a total burden," she admits, with a touch of sadness in both her tone and her posture.

My chest aches, painfully at merely the thought of her feeling like she doesn't belong here. I cringe, realizing I'm probably responsible for a lot of those feelings because of how I treated her when I first met her. I need to fix this, now. "Don't be silly. We always take in strays for holidays," I tease her, trying to lighten her mood.

"Excuse me?" she asks, obviously offended.

I wince and give a slight shake of my head. "That sounded bad. I didn't mean it like that," I insist, defensively.

"Then how did you mean it?" she challenges, with an arch of her eyebrow.

I heave a sigh and set the now empty plate down on the counter. I wipe off my hands on a napkin and toss it onto the plate. Then I lean back against the cabinets behind me and try to explain simply and honestly. She deserves at least that much. "Holidays have never been just me and my parents. Mom has been the mayor for a really long time and we constantly have people over for Christmas Eve, Christmas, Thanksgiving..." I trail off thoughtfully, before continuing. "You name it and people come over. She's the most popular person in the town," I announce, feeling a little bitter.

"It must be tough to share her," Ivy observes, watching me closely.

My eyes widen in surprise, but I downplay my feelings. I shrug and concede, "Sometimes, I guess." I sigh and continue, "My point is that we have an open door policy. We never turn anyone away."

"It's so different with my family," Ivy reveals, thoughtfully. "It was always just the four of us. We have really special traditions for the holidays," she adds.

"Don't get me wrong," I argue, "we have special traditions too."

"Maybe we can share some tomorrow?" Ivy suggests, smiling shyly.

I grin at her and nod my head. "Yeah, I'd like that," I happily admit.

I step slightly closer to her, not being able to take my eyes off her. There's just something about her that keeps pulling me in closer to her and wanting to really know her. The last thing I want to do is even try to get away. She looks intently into my eyes, leaning a little closer to me. I tip my head down towards her, wanting to kiss her.

My dad picks that moment to stride into the kitchen. He steps up to both of us with a broad smile. "Max!" he exclaims. "There you are."

Ivy startles and spins around quickly. She blushes a deep shade of red and begins fumbling with the spatula, as she moves more cookies over to an empty tray. I grin at how adorable she is when she's flustered. I shake my head at my dad, barely able to contain my laughter.

"Oh, did I interrupt something?" he inquires, as he looks back and forth between the two of us. He's probably only asking because of our odd reactions when he walked in the room.

"Nope, not at all," Ivy announces, awkwardly.

"You have the worst timing, Pops," I enlighten him, with a smirk and a slight shake of my head.

"What did I do?" he prods, confused.

Instead of answering him, I inform him, "I'm going to clean up and get changed. I'll be back shortly." I pat him on the shoulder and walk past him, heading for the stairs.

I make it upstairs without anyone else stopping me. I take a quick shower, anxious to get back downstairs to Ivy. I grin, chuckling to myself at Ivy's reaction when my dad walked into the room. He really does have horrible timing. I pull on a pair of nice jeans, a burgundy dress shirt and a black belt and black tie. I glance in the mirror one more time. I run my hands over my hair to smooth it out. Then I turn to make my way back downstairs.

As I walk down the stairs, my eyes immediately begin scanning the room, searching for Ivy. I spot her talking to Todd under the mistletoe, causing my jaw to clench in reaction. His brown hair is perfectly styled and he's wearing dark jeans and a gray sweater with a zipper at his neck, pulled halfway down. He's smiling from ear to ear, as he looks down at her, as if he's ready to pounce. My stomach churns, anxiously and I gulp down the growing lump in my throat. "I'm not jealous," I grumble, irritably to myself. Ivy glances up in my direction, before she brings her focus back to Todd. I walk over so I'm standing near them, hoping to hear some of their conversation, but I don't want to be rude and interrupt...yet. One of my mom's friends stops me to say, "Hello." I smile stiffly and nod in greeting, my attention completely focused on Ivy.

"I didn't even notice," she admits, kindly. "I was just handing out food to guests," she informs him. She points to the empty tray she just set down on the small accent table along the wall.

He nods in acknowledgement, before he continues. "Well, you have to kiss someone under the mistletoe, or it's eight years bad luck," Todd educates her, causing my blood to heat.

Ivy giggles, the sweet sound making my stomach twist anxiously. "I've never heard that before. Is that a Pennsylvania tradition or something?" she questions.

"No," he shakes his head, "I don't think so. I think it's from London," he replies.

"I'm surprised it's not Paris," Ivy jokes.

"Paris?" Todd asks, sounding confused.

"Well, it is the city of love," she adds, playfully.

Is she flirting? She sounds like she's flirting, which only succeeds in pushing me over the edge. I clench my jaw and take a deep breath to try to calm myself down, but I just can't take anymore. In two long strides, I step in between the two of them, without a greeting. I barely glance upwards and point at the mistletoe, before I remark, "Hey, mistletoe!" I wrap my arms around Ivy and dip her slightly towards the ground, away from Todd. Her eyes widen and she reflexively holds onto my arms. I kiss her, not giving her a chance to push me away, or to kiss anyone else. I spin her back to her feet and she stares at me shocked, her mouth slightly open. I leave my arm draped over her shoulders and possessively pull her a little closer to me.

I notice the moment she pulls herself together. Her eyes narrow on me just before she yells my name, "Max!"

"Hey, man. Merry Christmas!" Todd grumbles, to get my attention.

I glance over to him, as if I just realized he was standing there. "Merry Christmas, Todd," I tell him, pasting a fake smile on my face. "How's your fiancé?" I inquire.

Ivy looks over to Todd with wide eyes, appearing flustered, giving me the reaction I was hoping for. He smirks and gives me a knowing look. Then, he gladly announces, "We broke up."

I frown and grumble, "Oh."

He winks at Ivy and grins. "Maybe some other time," he suggests.

Ivy is too stunned to speak, but I glower at him until he spots someone else across the room. He holds his hand up and waves, "Hey, Julie! When am I going to get you under the mistletoe?" He strides away, crossing the room towards Julie and I feel my whole body sigh with relief.

I drop my arm from around Ivy. Then, I call out to Todd, "Enjoy the party!"

I feel Ivy move suddenly. She plants her hands on my side and shoves me away from her, defiantly. I look down at her and wince at the glare she's focusing on me. "I can't believe you!" she declares, vehemently.

"What?" I ask, innocently.

"You know what," she insists.

"He was going to try to kiss you," I explain, attempting to get her to see reason.

"You kissed me," she emphasizes.

"Yeah, so?" I prompt. I know it was our first kiss, but we've almost kissed a couple times already. It shouldn't be that big of a deal.

"I didn't say you could kiss me," she proclaims, insolently.

I huff a humorless laugh and pinch the bridge of my nose in frustration. "But he's a stranger," I argue, stunned we're having this conversation.

"You're a stranger, too, Max," she claims.

I flinch at her words and grind my jaw in irritation. "No, I'm not. You at least know my name," I reply bitterly. Did she want to kiss him?

"I knew his name," she states, defensively.

"Yeah?" I probe, with an arch of my eyebrow. I cross my arms over my chest and challenge her. "What was it?"

She crosses her arms over her chest, mirroring me. She innocently answers, "Todd."

I shake my head in annoyance. "You only knew it because I said it," I remind her.

"So?" she argues, with a shrug.

I take a deep breath and grind my jaw in annoyance. Then I quietly mumble, "I didn't mean to offend you, Ivy. I'm sorry."

"Sorry for..." she prompts.

I grimace and grumble, "I'm sorry for kissing you."

She gasps, her face registering both hurt and shock. Then, she asks with incredulity dripping from her voice, "Oh, so you're sorry for kissing me?"

I throw my arms up in the air and grunt in frustration. "Sheesh, you're impossible!" I complain. I don't know what she wants me to say. "I'm sorry for kissing you without your permission. Okay?" I push, completely exasperated.

Ivy smiles smugly, pulling a laugh out of me. "Yes," she agrees. "Apology accepted."

I look up at the mistletoe and give a slight shake of my head. She's unbelievable. "It's a silly tradition anyway," I concede, with a sigh.

Her eyebrows draw down in confusion, before turning to surprise. She questions, "He was telling the truth?"

"About eight years of bad luck if you don't kiss someone under the mistletoe?" I clarify. She nods in confirmation. "Yes, of course," I reply, simply.

"Oh," she mumbles and pauses. "Well, I wouldn't want us to have bad luck," she claims. She twists a little at her waist, her dress swinging slightly. She glances up at me from underneath her long lashes, causing my heartbeat to quicken.

I bite my lower lip, so I don't laugh at her instant change in attitude. I grin down at her and play along. "Oh, no, that would be awful. I've been so lucky in love too," I comment, sarcastically.

"Yeah, so have I," she agrees, echoing my sarcastic tone and smiling adorably.

"Which is why I kissed you," I claim, even though we both know it's not true. "I don't want eight more years of bad luck," I announce, fighting a smile.

"Me neither," she murmurs.

"Especially in love," I emphasize.

"Right," she agrees.

"We're still under the mistletoe, you know," I remind her, glancing up above our heads. Then, I move a little closer to her.

She blushes a beautiful shade of pink and grins up at me. "I see that," she acknowledges.

We both burst out laughing. When we stop and catch our breath, we move even closer together. I lean in, feeling so drawn to her. We pause, barely a breath apart, staring into each other's eyes. I begin to close the final distance between us, when she quickly pushes up on her toes and turns her head to the side at the last second, kissing me on the cheek. "Merry Christmas, Max," she whispers.

She falls back on her heels and smiles up at me, her blue eyes sparkling. I grin down at her and repeat her sentiment, "Merry Christmas." I watch her walk away as I chuckle to myself. I give my head a light shake, trying to comprehend what just happened. She's really going to drive me crazy, but I have to admit, I like it. I like her. I reluctantly tear my eyes away from Ivy's retreating form. I take a deep breath, not able to wipe the smile off my face. Then, I force myself to make my way around the room to greet everyone, like I know my mom would want me to do.

Chapter 15

Max

It's the end of the night and to say I'm thankful to see the last of our family, friends and neighbors leave is an understatement. It's been a long couple of days, but also pretty incredible ones too. More than anything, I want to talk to Ivy. I just can't talk to her the way I really need to with literally the whole town in my house. Then on top of everything, she was upset with me about how I reacted to the Todd situation. I grind my teeth getting angry all over again, just thinking about him attempting to steal *my* kiss from Ivy under the mistletoe. I don't blame him. She did look absolutely gorgeous tonight. But I couldn't let Todd be the one to kiss her. I needed to be the one to kiss her. I would do exactly what I did tonight if I had to do it all over again. At least she wasn't upset with me for very long, but now I want to talk to her even more. I need to tell her what's really been going through my head. If I wait too long, I may miss my chance.

I heave a sigh, as we all begin cleaning up. I don't think any of us want to worry about cleaning tomorrow on Christmas Eve. Hopefully, we won't have to think about anything except celebrating the holiday together. Unfortunately, both of my parents are barely able to keep their eyes open. I easily convince both my mom and dad to go to bed. Although, I think my mom's reasons might have nothing to do with being exhausted and more to do with leaving Ivy and me alone. "I promise, Mom. Ivy and I will just finish up in here. Then, we'll go upstairs to sleep. We don't want to wake up and have to do dishes and clean up the garbage. I'd rather do it tonight," I insist.

"Are you sure?" she questions.

I nod my head in confirmation as Ivy verbally agrees, "We're sure, Judy. We've got the last of this."

"Okay," she concedes, nodding at Ivy.

I step up to her and place a kiss on her head. "We'll go right up to bed after we finish this up," I reiterate.

She yawns and then wraps her arms around me, giving me a hug. "Alright," she repeats. "Goodnight, Max."

"Goodnight, Mom," I softly murmur and try to guide her up the stairs.

""Goodnight, Ivy," she calls. "Thank you again for everything. Everything was just perfect," she emphasizes.

"I'm glad," she grins in satisfaction. "Goodnight, Judy," Ivy responds. Then, she ambles towards the kitchen carrying more dirty dishes. My mom walks upstairs and Ivy reemerges from the kitchen a moment later to grab more food trays. I reach for another garbage bag and quickly force myself to get moving so we can finish. We're able to work pretty quickly to get everything looking neat and clean again. I notice Ivy take the last of the food trays back into the kitchen, while I hurry to finish picking up the last of the garbage in the dining room.

A few minutes later, Ivy walks back in from the kitchen and immediately flops down on the couch in the sitting area near me. "All done. Your mom will wake up to a sparkling clean kitchen," she announces, sounding both pleased and exhausted. She slips her shoes off and drops them gently on the floor.

"Yup," I agree. "This is the last of it. The rest of the house is clean," I announce. I tie off the black garbage bag in my hands and walk over to set it by the door, ready to take out. I appreciatively mumble, "Thanks for helping, Ivy."

"Oh, it's fine," she claims, blowing off my compliment, as if it were no big deal. But everything she did for my mom, for me, for my family, its all a big deal to me. "It helped me keep my mind off my family anyway," she admits, as she absentmindedly smooths down her dress.

I flinch, my heart clenching, painfully with her confession. I can't help but imagine what it's like for her to be so far away from her family for Christmas, especially when she had planned on being with them. I'll probably never say it to her, but now that I know her better, I understand why she was trying to drive home. I honestly think I would've done the exact same thing if I were in her situation. "You really miss them, huh?" I gently prompt.

She nods her head, solemnly and admits, "I do." She glances up at me and forces a smile. "I haven't seen them since the summer," she acknowledges, as if she just had that realization, but I don't believe for a second she had to think about how long it has been since she's seen her family. Even when I was living in Manhattan, I never had to be away for that long, but I understand sometimes you have to do what you can. Plus, Charleston is a lot farther away.

I stride over to her and place my hands on the back of the couch. I lean in towards her and ask, "You didn't go home for Thanksgiving?"

"I couldn't," she concedes, with a small shake of her head. "The restaurant had a big event and I couldn't miss it," she informs me.

"Your family didn't come down?" I question, surprised.

She gives another small shake of her head and attempts to hide how much it bothers her, but I see right through her barriers. "No, my dad broke his ankle skiing.

It was too much, so we made plans for Christmas," she explains, unsuccessfully trying to keep the emotion out of her voice.

"What about Sawyer?" I prompt. I watch her face closely as her emotions go through her, before she instantly attempts to stifle them, as I make my way around to the other side of the couch. I know how close she is to her brother.

"He stayed home to help. Dad was sad enough not having me there," she acknowledges. "Sawyer didn't want to make it worse and I didn't either," she relents.

I grimace, feeling even worse for the way I treated her the day I found her stranded on the side of the road, if that's possible. I honestly don't know what to do, except give her comfort any way I can. I gulp down the lump in my throat and sincerely convey, "I'm really sorry, Ivy." I sit down next to her on the couch and without thinking I offer, "I can try to get you home tomorrow." I just want to do something in an attempt to cheer her up and help her get what she deserves for Christmas. Why should she have to miss another holiday with her family if I can do something about it? I honestly think I might do anything to help her.

She grins, politely, but waves me off, "Don't be silly. Tomorrow is Christmas Eve. There aren't any flights."

"I can try to drive you," I suggest. "The truck is pretty powerful," I remind her, with a playful smirk.

She giggles and then gives me a look as if I've lost my mind. Then again, even I realize my complete one-eighty when it comes to Ivy. But I really should have treated her this way from the start. "Even if the snow isn't as bad as they say it's going to be, why should you miss Christmas with your parents?" she probes.

My stomach does a flip, hearing her put me before herself. I can't hide my broad smile, as I feel my face heat. "You know, I think I might prefer to spend it with you," I admit, realizing the truth in my words the moment they leave my mouth.

I hear her slight gasp of surprise. Then, she pauses before she insists, "Well, I'm not going anywhere. You can spend it with me here."

I instantly feel a wave of relief wash over me from my head to my toes, both inside and out. I don't want her to leave. I gulp over the lump in my throat and try to lighten the mood. "And..." I hesitate before I ask, "You're really cooking for us?" I don't want her to think her agreeing to cook Christmas Eve dinner is the only reason I want her here because that would be the furthest thing from the truth. I will admit it's definitely a really sweet bonus, though.

She hides her smile behind her hand. Then, she squares her shoulders and answers me with confidence. "Yes. Absolutely," she confirms.

The corners of my lips twitch up in anticipation. "Now, that's what I'm really looking forward to," I tease her. She giggles in response, the light sound giving me goosebumps. "As long as there aren't any emergencies, I'll be able to stay home all day," I inform her, loving the idea of being able to spend all of Christmas Eve with her tomorrow.

Ivy rests her head back on her arm and leans into the back of the couch. I can't help but admire her as she closes her eyes, a small smile lighting up her face. "Mm," she murmurs, sleepily. "Sounds nice," she ponders.

I take a deep breath and lean forward, resting my elbows on my knees. I look down at my hands and begin fidgeting nervously. I have to tell her how I'm feeling before I lose my chance. I glance back at her again, admiring her soft profile and then I focus back on my hands. Now that we're finally alone, this is the perfect time to finally talk to her. I've been waiting all day for this time with her. Now, I just have to get it out, I remind myself for encouragement. "I need to get something off my chest, Ivy," I finally admit.

"Mm hmm," she prompts.

I take another deep, calming breath and exhale slowly to get rid of my nerves, before I begin talking. "Last night, I didn't know it was you that was here. George told me that Mom took a stranger home and I left before I could get any other details," I grimace. "I thought you were a hitchhiker or something," I confess, still feeling a little guilty for barging in on her unexpectedly the other night. "My mom is known to do that. You know, take strangers in because she feels bad for them, especially around the holidays," I mumble in attempt to explain my foolishness.

"Then, when I saw you in those silly pajamas," I huff a laugh and give a slight shake of my head, "I was so relieved," I breathe a sigh of relief. "But I also couldn't believe it was you. I didn't think I'd ever see you again and I didn't want to," I concede, regretfully. I pause and take another calming breath before I'm able to continue.

"My heart was broken pretty badly a few years ago and it has taken me a long time to get over it," I disclose. "But when I saw you under the mistletoe with Todd," I begin, feeling my whole body tense. I grind my teeth and shake my head in annoyance just thinking about it. "I don't know what came over me," I grumble, irritably. "Jealousy, I think," I concede. "I got so mad thinking that you were going to kiss him. I wanted to kiss you," I emphasize, "so I did," I declare, simply. "When I kissed you," I pause, nervous and trying to find the right words.

140

"When we kissed," I start over, "I felt something," I finally blurt out. "Did you?" I ask, hopeful.

I wring my hands together, anxiously awaiting her answer, but she remains silent. I know she didn't kiss me back, but I just thought I took her by surprise. Does she really not feel the same way? I finally force myself to spin around, steeling myself to meet her gaze and preparing to hear whatever she has to say. "Ivy?" I prompt. I take in her closed eyes and the awkward flop of her head against the back of the couch. I chuckle and shake my head in disbelief. Of course! I finally open myself up and tell her how I'm feeling and she falls asleep before she can hear what I have to say. I heave a sigh, knowing I'm going to have to do this all over again.

I stand up and scoop her off the couch. I hold her in my arms and she instinctively wraps her arms around my neck and nuzzles into my chest. My heartbeat speeds up and my body instantly warms having her so close. I pause to take a deep breath to calm myself down. I turn and slowly carry her up the stairs, as her small body bounces lightly against me with each step I take. I lean down to push down on the door handle and with a gentle nudge of my shoulder on the door; I make my way into the spare bedroom. I walk over to the side of the bed and carefully lay her down, but she's so tired, she doesn't wake up or even move an inch. I cover her up with a blanket and stare down at her, admiring her beauty.

My heart feels like it's ready to explode with how much I already care for her. How did this even happen? I gently push her hair back out of her face, allowing my fingers to briefly trail along her cheek. I smile down at her, admiring her beauty and loving how incredibly peaceful she looks sound asleep. I'm truly thankful she crashed into my life, almost literally. Now, I'm hoping we find a way for her to remain a part of it. I cautiously back away, trying not to wake her. I flip off the light, before soundlessly pulling the door closed behind me. "Goodnight, Ivy," I whisper outside her door. I heave a sigh and stride across the hall towards my own room, hoping to get some sleep. I'm definitely tired enough, but can I stop thinking about Ivy long enough to start dreaming?

Chapter 16

Ivy

"I love you too," I proclaim, just before I end the call with my mom and dad. Then, I drop the phone on the bed and walk into the bathroom to finish getting ready. I pull a teal cable-knit sweater on over my head and pull it down over my black leggings. I look at myself in the mirror, while I quickly pull my hair into a low bun, leaving a few strands hanging down in front. I can't stop thinking about last night, as I begin putting on my make-up. I keep imagining Max's' arms around me, carrying me upstairs to my room, but it feels more like a dream than reality. It must've happened, though, because I woke up in my bed this morning on top of the covers. My dress was still on and I was covered up with a soft, warm blanket. I can't help but smile to myself as I think about him taking care of me.

Then there's the fact that he kissed me last night and I decided to argue with him about it. I really don't understand why I did that, except for the fact that he took me completely off-guard. I grimace, just thinking about my reaction. I'm so frustrated with myself because I did want to kiss him. I still want to kiss him. I sigh and shake my head at myself. I can admit that maybe I like pushing his buttons, just like he pushes mine. I like the banter back and forth between us. There's something about him that helps me feel energized, empowered and confident when he's around. Plus, I get chills just thinking about him.

I quickly finish my make-up. Then, I place the last of my make-up brushes on the sink with a sigh. I give myself one last look in the mirror. I add a little bit more lipstick, before deciding I'm ready to go downstairs.

I head to the kitchen, hoping I'm up early enough to make breakfast. I want to do something for Max that says, thank you for taking such good care of me last night. I thought doing something to take care of him this morning would help reciprocate and hopefully show him how special he's becoming to me, too. I walk into the kitchen to find Judy starting the first pot of coffee. "Good morning," I announce, greeting her cheerfully.

She turns and smiles, her cheeks rosy with the burgundy mock turtleneck shirt she's wearing. "Good morning, Ivy. Did you sleep well?" she inquires.

I nod in confirmation and reply, "Yes, thank you." I pause a moment before I request, "Do you mind if I make breakfast this morning?"

Her eyes widen in surprise, "Really? You already did so much last night," she reiterates. "Plus, you said you wanted to cook dinner tonight," she reminds me, making sure that's what I really want to do.

I nod in agreement, "I do want to cook tonight, but I'd also love to make breakfast this morning for all of you too," I insist. I don't want to explain to Max's parents that I want to make breakfast to do something special for him. "How about Pancakes and sausage?" I suggest.

She grins and nods her head. "Okay," she concedes. "I'll cut up some fruit to go with it," she offers.

Charles enters at the tail end of the conversation, wearing gray sweatpants and an olive green t-shirt. He asks, "Did I hear you say pancakes?" I look up at him and nod in confirmation. He grins, "I love pancakes."

I giggle at his childlike response and greet him, "Good morning, Charles."

"Good morning, Ivy," he responds. "Good morning, Sweetheart," he adds, giving Judy a quick, good morning kiss.

"Good morning," she replies, smiling up at him. She walks over to the refrigerator and pulls out strawberries, blueberries, as well as some cantaloupe and honeydew melon. Then, she reaches in one of the lower cabinets to pull out a cutting board, before grabbing a chef's knife and a utility knife out of the bamboo knife block. She easily cleans all the berries. Then, she swiftly cuts up all of the fruit and mixes it together in a large serving bowl.

I immediately get to work on the pancakes, warming up the griddle, while I make the homemade batter. Then, I place the sausage links in another pan on the stove to cook. Judy finishes her task quickly and offers, "Is there anything else I can do to help?"

"Why don't the two of you sit and have coffee," I suggest. "I can take care of the rest," I insist.

"Thank you, Ivy," Judy smiles, appreciatively. She pours the rest of the coffee into a silver coffee pot and places it on the counter. Then, she sits down next to Charles.

"That was a wonderful party last night," I murmur. "Thank you."

Judy and Charles both chuckle. "It was a wonderful party last night because of you," Judy maintains, causing me to blush. "I should be the one thanking you," she emphasizes.

I shrug, like it's no big deal. "I told you before, I was happy to help. I really had fun," I admit, honestly. I flip the first few pancakes onto plates for them, along with some sausage. I walk a plate over to each of them, setting them down on the counter in front of them. "Enjoy," I announce, happily.

"Thank you," they both reply, in unison. I move back to the stove and fill my own plate, glancing anxiously at the doorway every few seconds.

I exhale slowly, feeling my shoulders relax the moment I see Max trudging into the kitchen. He's wearing a blue t-shirt with dark and light blue-checkered flannel pajama pants. He looks absolutely adorable with his hair rumpled from sleep, causing tingles to spread throughout my body. He covers his mouth from a yawn. I smile broadly, excited to see him. I struggle to hold some of my emotions back, and hope I don't appear too eager. "Good morning!" I greet him.

He gives me a tired smile as his green eyes meet mine. He replies with a deep, groggy, morning voice, "Morning."

"Coffee?" I offer.

He nods his head and pleads, "Please."

I pour him a cup of coffee and bring it over to him. He smiles his thank you. Then, I prod, "Breakfast?"

He gives a slight shake of his head and replies, "Not right now. I need to wake up first." I feel a slight tinge of disappointment, but I'm sure he'll have some soon. He leans down and kisses his mom on the top of her head, making me smile to myself. I love how close he is to his family. Since family is so important to me, knowing he feels the same way really means a lot to me. I walk over to the stove and grab the plate I just filled and set it down on the end of the counter before I sit down.

"Morning, Max," his mom smiles up at him.

"Morning," he rasps, as he finally lowers himself onto a stool at the counter, right next to me. My body heats instantly with our close proximity. "How is it outside?" he questions.

Charles grimaces and sets his fork down before he announces, "Got another six inches dumped on us last night."

"When is this snow going to stop already?" Max prods, in exasperation. "It has to be some sort of record," he grumbles.

Charles nods his head in agreement, "It is. It's the biggest snow storm to hit us since 1961," he adds.

"My dad said that it's supposed to stop in Boston tonight around eight," I apprise them, passing on the information my dad shared with me this morning.

Charles nods slowly, thinking about my statement. "That sounds about right. It's supposed to stop here around two or so," he updates us.

Max turns to me and inquires, "Are you sure you don't want me to get you home?"

My heart warms at his offer. I nod and offer him a grateful smile. "I'm sure," I confirm. I pause as an unsettling feeling plants itself in my gut, causing my stomach to churn. I gulp down the sudden lump in my throat and arch my eyebrows in challenge. "Unless you're trying to get rid of me?" I question, steeling myself for his answer.

"Of course not!" Judy exclaims, not giving Max a chance to respond.

I add, "Besides, there are no flights into Logan Airport today or tomorrow. I can start driving after Christmas breakfast," I tell them. I hope that's okay with Max.

Max's shoulders slouch and he grimaces slightly. "Oh. Yeah, I guess the roads will be clear by then," he mumbles.

Charles grimaces and sighs in defeat. He looks up and gives me a look full of regret, ready to share some news I'm not sure I want to hear. "Ivy, it may take a little longer than a couple of days. You've got a broken axel," he informs me.

Max grins at his dad's announcement, completely confusing me. Why is that good news? "What does that mean?" I question, thinking maybe I misunderstood his meaning. It's not like I know anything about cars.

Max turns towards me and happily answers my question. "It means your wheels won't turn until we fix it," he announces.

I look down at my plate, my heart suddenly aching to see my family, knowing I have no way of getting home anytime soon. I mumble, "Oh."

"Don't worry, Princess," Max encourages. "We'll take good care of you," he proclaims.

I look up at him from underneath my eyelashes and smile, my heart now clenching for a different reason.

I notice a knowing look pass between Judy and Charles and quickly change the subject. I don't want anyone's pity. "So," I begin, "what are your Christmas traditions?" I question.

Judy grins and claims, "We have a few."

"Like what?" I prompt, curiously.

"Well," Charles begins, the corners of his mouth twitching up in amusement, "on Christmas Eve, we all wear matching Christmas pajamas."

I laugh and Max groans in annoyance, giving his dad a disgruntled look. "I am not doing that this year," he insists.

"Hey, it's only fair, since you saw me in my Christmas PJ's," I murmur grinning.

"Yeah, what are those all about anyway?" he questions, smirking at me. He's obviously trying to pull the attention away from himself, but I allow it to happen, giving him a short reprieve.

148

"My family has a pajama tradition too," I announce. Max arches his eyebrows in question and waits for me to continue. "We see who can wear the most Christmas-spirited PJ's. We've been doing it since Sawyer and I were teenagers. No one sees each other's pajamas until Christmas breakfast," I explain.

Max chuckles, his eyes sparkling with laughter. "Yeah, I bet you would have won this year," he replies, with confidence.

I square my shoulders and proudly announce, "I'm the reigning champ! Although my dad does give me a run for my money every now and again."

Max chuckles and adds one of his favorite traditions. "Mom usually bakes my favorite Christmas cookies every year," Max declares, with a lick of his lips.

"Just so we can leave some for Santa, right Max?" Judy prompts, sweetly. Max rolls his eyes, but maintains his wide grin.

"He has a special glass for milk too," Charles adds.

I giggle, remembering yesterday when he kept declaring nearly every cookie as his favorite. "What kind of cookies?" I ask, curiously.

"Chocolate chip, of course," he states, as if my question was ridiculous.

"Ooh, a traditionalist," I tease. I'm really enjoying learning so much about him.

He nods in agreement. "Yeah, but those lemon drop cookies that you made are a close second," he proclaims, licking his lips as if he can taste them.

I grin, pleased he liked my cookies so much. "Why, thank you," I mumble, grateful.

"Hint-hint," he jokes, bumping me playfully in the side with his elbow.

I laugh and smile brightly at him. "I got it. I'll make some more today," I concede.

"Good! I only got two last night," he reveals.

"We had barely any leftovers," Charles announces.

"I'm so glad that everyone enjoyed the food," I state, proudly.

"I don't know how I can repay you, Ivy," Judy admits in awe.

My eyes widen and I probe, "Are you kidding?" I'm shocked she would say something like that. "You gave me a place to stay for Christmas," I remind her.

"That's what Christmas is all about, isn't it?" she prompts.

I nod and concur, "It is." I pause and then continue, "So what about you, Judy? What's your favorite Christmas tradition?"

Judy, Max and Charles all answer the question in unison, "Getting dressed up on Christmas."

Judy laughs in disbelief, her mouth dropping slightly open. "Oh, come on! Am I that predictable?" she questions, glancing back and forth between her husband and her son.

Charles holds his thumb and pointer finger close together and admits with a teasing grin, "A little." She chuckles and smiles back at him.

I question, "Where do you go?"

Judy's eyebrows draw together in confusion and she asks, "What do you mean?"

"Well, you get all dressed up..." I pause before repeating my question, "Where do you go?"

"We don't go anywhere," Max states and shrugs his shoulders.

"Really?" I ask, my surprise evident.

Judy nods in confirmation and elaborates, "I grew up in Manhattan and it's something that my family always did."

"We kept the tradition after we got married," Charles adds.

"We go to Church in the afternoon, but that's about it," Judy concedes.

"Mom usually cooks a big Christmas dinner and then we all sit in our best Christmas clothes and enjoy it," Max expounds.

"I love that," I tell them, sincerely. "And I actually packed the perfect outfit to wear," I announce, with a satisfied grin.

"Okay," Judy agrees. Then she suggests, "One more tradition. Something special from you and your family," she requests.

"We make Christmas wishes," I answer immediately, remembering one of my favorite family traditions.

"How do you do that?" Max questions.

"Well," I begin, "everyone gets a slip of paper and a marker. We sit in front of the fireplace with hot cocoa and we write our Christmas wish on the paper. Then, we fold it up and put it in front of the fireplace. If you're really good, your wish will get sucked up into the chimney and make its way to Santa's sleigh," I explain. I end with a smile, as holiday memories from through the years run through my mind.

"Really?" Max asks, arching his eyebrow.

I blush and shrug my shoulders. "Well, maybe not, but the heat sometimes mixes with the cool air at the top of the chimney and creates a little vacuum. My dad is a science teacher. He probably figured it out and came up with the tradition," I concede.

"That's adorable," Judy praises.

"I think we should do it tonight," Charles suggests.

I smile grateful. "Really?" I ask, my excitement apparent. All three of them nod in agreement. "Okay. After dinner," I confirm, in delight.

Max looks at me and holds my gaze, causing my heart to race. Then, he announces, "It's a date." He smiles broadly sending chills of anticipation down my spine.

Chapter 17

Max

I saunter into the sitting room, stepping around the two cream armchairs covered with thin flowers in shades of yellow and brown, and walk right up to the elongated bay window. I lean against the windowsill and cross my arms over my chest. I peer outside at all the snow, the blue of my sweatshirt almost giving the white snow a bluish hue. I wouldn't care what color the snow appeared to be if it didn't go anywhere and we were all stuck here together for a while longer. I want, no, I need more time with Ivy. She drives me crazy, but that's just because she's a beautiful, strong, independent woman, who challenges me more than anyone has ever done before. That also sounds like a list of some of the things I really like about her. All I want to do is pull her closer to me and find out everything I can about her. I want to know all her likes and dislikes, what makes her laugh or cry, what her interests are outside of cooking and her family. I also want to know more about her family and what it was like for her growing up with a twin brother. Plus, I want her to have the time to see the man that I am. I'm not ready for her to leave. I cringe just thinking about it.

I wish I could figure out a way to convince her to stay, even for just a little while longer. Maybe I could persuade dad to take his time fixing her car, but that won't necessarily keep her here once the roads and airport open up again. I have to consider she might leave another way, even without her car. Then again, if she did, she would have to come back at another time to pick up her car and I would have the chance to see her again. I grimace, the moment I realize she could also send someone else to pick her car up for her. I groan in frustration and run a hand down my face, keen for this storm to continue.

I'm willing to admit to myself that I'm afraid if she leaves now, before we have more time together, I might not ever see her again. My heart clenches tightly at the thought, making it hard to breathe. I close my eyes and take a deep breath to calm my pounding heart. I shake my head, refusing to consider her leaving for good before we are able to figure this out together. Which only brings me back to the same question I've been asking myself almost constantly since I realized Ivy was staying at our house for the duration of the storm. "What am I going to do?" I grumble to myself, feeling exasperated.

"Here you go, Max," my dad announces, as he strides into the sitting room, interrupting my thoughts of Ivy.

I drop my arms to my sides and push away from the wall, as I turn around to acknowledge him. He's wearing his typical blue jeans and flannel shirt, this one white and gray, but what he's carrying grabs my attention and causes the corners of my lips to curve up. He's holding two plates, one in each hand and both with delicious looking sandwiches on them. "What's this?" I prompt. My stomach growls in anticipation and I'm suddenly starving. He places both plates on the small accent table between the two chairs, right next to the windows.

"Lunch," he happily proclaims. "A Chicken Parm Panini," he informs me. He grins proudly at the food, as if he made the sandwich for me himself, but I know better than to believe that. He takes a seat in one of the swivel armchairs next to me.

I close my eyes momentarily and take a deep breath in through my nose, inhaling the delicious scent. My taste buds water as the tomato based scent, along with oregano, basil, garlic and other Italian spices hits my nose. I'm pretty sure I already know the answer, but I ask anyway, wanting confirmation. "Made by..." I prod, dragging out the words.

"Ivy," he answers, simply.

I can't help the wide grin that instantly covers my face. I place my hands on the knees of my jeans as I lower myself into the chair across from my dad and spin myself inwards towards the table. I immediately pick up one of the hearty sandwiches with both hands, completely famished. I open my mouth and take a large bite, while my dad mirrors my movements with his own food.

"Mm," I groan in appreciation. "Man," I mumble around the food in my mouth, "that girl can cook!" I exclaim.

My dad nods his head in agreement. "And how," he mutters, appreciatively, around his own sandwich.

I take a sip of the water from the glass on the table in front of me. Then, I hold it up with a confused look on my face. "Where did this come from?" I question.

He chuckles, "I set them down just before I went back to the kitchen for the sandwiches. You were really deep in thought," he explains. "I didn't want to interrupt right away," he adds, with a casual shrug. Then, he takes another bite.

I chuckle and shake my head at myself. He's right. I was really deep in thought. I'm not really surprised I didn't hear him come in before. Thoughts of Ivy seem to consume nearly all of my attention since the moment I met her and it only seems to be getting worse the more I get to know her. I have to figure out what to do before my opportunity disappears. I've already gotten a second chance from her after treating her so rudely. I can't imagine her giving me a third. I glance up at my dad and then curiously towards the kitchen, where Ivy is with my mom, before focusing back on him. I've always been able to talk to him about anything and everything. It's one of the reasons we've always been so close and why this past year was so tough. I should be able to talk to him about this too. "Mom and Ivy are still cooking dinner?" I inquire.

He nods in confirmation and mumbles, "Yup."

"So they'll be busy for a while, right?" I prompt, anxiously.

"I'd say so," he agrees.

"Good," I mumble, as a relieved sigh escapes through my lips. Now that I know Ivy and Mom probably won't be leaving the kitchen any time soon, I can talk to him without one of them overhearing me, before I'm ready to share everything with Ivy. I have to talk to someone. I set my sandwich down on my plate and begin fidgeting with my hands, anticipating this upcoming conversation. "Dad, I want to talk to you about something," I request, vaguely.

"Go for it," he encourages. Then he brings his sandwich to his mouth and takes another bite, continuing to eat.

I pause, trying to organize my thoughts, before I tell him what I've been thinking. I take a deep breath, attempting to gather the courage to admit my feelings for Ivy to my Dad. I remind myself, this shouldn't be any different than talking to him in the past. But, it does feel different because Ivy's special. I square my shoulders and force myself to open my mouth and speak. "When you met mom, did you know right away that she was the one?" I blurt out, curiously.

Dad instantly starts coughing and puts his hand over his mouth. With his eyes wide, he attempts to catch his breath. He stops coughing and tries to finish chewing the food in his mouth before speaking. That wasn't the reaction I was expecting, but I guess it's understandable. I continue, anxiously, not able to wait another second for an answer from him. "I mean, I'm not running down the aisle or anything, but there's just something about Ivy," I divulge, attempting to explain how she makes me feel. "There's just something between us I've never felt before. I didn't even feel it with Bridget," I admit. I grimace at the reminder of my ex-girlfriend.

"Ugh," he grumbles, his mouth still full.

"I know, I know," I groan. "Bridget came at a tough time," I wince again. "And after everything she did to me, I shouldn't even compare how I felt about her to how I feel about Ivy, but…" I trail off, struggling to put my thoughts and feelings into words. I just want him to understand and I really am just trying to figure out how to convey it to him. It's just extremely hard to do when I'm still trying to understand it all myself. I just know in my heart it's something truly big. But if I can't explain it to him, how will I ever tell Ivy? "This is different, Dad. Ivy is different," I emphasize. "She challenges me in a good way. She's got a fire in her, you know?" I question, a smile touching my lips.

He takes another bite of his sandwich and nods his head in acknowledgement. "Mmph," he murmurs, with a mouthful.

I grin, thinking about Ivy doing what she can to give me a hard time. "I know. I like it too," I admit. "She's just so different than anyone else I've ever met," I insist.

"Mm hmm," dad nods again in agreement.

"And I love how close she is to her family," I continue, hearing the building excitement in my own voice. "You never see that anymore. I sometimes think I'm the only person my age that would drop anything for their parents and here she is trying to drive through a blizzard, just to get to her family for Christmas Eve," I murmur, with obvious admiration.

"Mmph," he mumbles, around another mouthful.

I nod in agreement, "Yeah, it was pretty stupid, but she's strong-willed. I like that," I proclaim. "She goes after what she wants and I'm pretty sure she'll get it," I declare, with complete confidence. "Mom said she's single, so maybe there's a chance…" I begin, feeling optimistic, as I trail off. My heart skips a beat at the possibility of really having a chance with her. I think we could be really good for each other, but I still need more time for us to really get to know each other and spend some time together, just the two of us.

"Mm," he hums in agreement.

I wince as I'm brought back to the reality of the driving distance between us, whether she's in Charleston or Boston, she's definitely not around the corner from Bethlehem, Pennsylvania. There has to be something we could do to make it work, so we would be able to see each other. I sigh sadly and concede, "I know the distance could be a deal breaker, but she said she wants to leave Charleston. Maybe she'll find something in Philly," I suggest, with a hopeful smile. An idea suddenly pops into my head and I gasp. I immediately blurt out my thoughts, my excitement obvious. "Could you imagine if she moved here and took over Blakely's Pub? That would be amazing," I stress. I can't stop myself from dreaming of being able to see her every single day.

"Mmph," he mutters, smiling around his sandwich. He nods his head and continues chewing, before taking another bite.

158

"She could do the cooking cause we all know she's a fantastic cook," I proclaim, confidently. He nods his head in agreement and continues eating. "And I could do the business end of it," I suggest. I love the idea of getting back into the business side of things. That's the one thing I really do miss since I left Manhattan. Besides, it's not like I would ever be able to take over for my dad, I don't know anything about cars, except the basics. But the thought of Ivy and I starting a restaurant business like this together is exhilarating. "I mean, we seem to get along pretty well. And if she feels the same way about me that I feel about her, well, then, maybe this could be something long term. Right?" I prompt, wanting confirmation from my dad that this could work for us. I suddenly feel incredibly optimistic about Ivy and me having a chance.

"Mm hmm," he agrees.

I have some work to do if I want to figure this out. I can eat upstairs in my room while I work. I grab the plate with my sandwich in one hand and my water in the other and stand up. "I'm going to do some research," I announce. "You never know," I declare with a wide grin, my confidence growing by the second.

"K," he mumbles, as he continues eating.

I smile at him, loving how much he's enjoying Ivy's sandwich. That alone is a testament to the fact that she should have her own restaurant. It's almost like he's never had anything so delicious before. You wouldn't think my mom could cook with his reaction, but she's a wonderful cook as well. To put it simply, it's just that I believe Ivy is better, but I'm not about to tell my mom that. I grin; satisfied, knowing this could work. I just have to figure out the details. "Good talk, Dad. Thanks," I mutter, appreciatively. I quickly stride out of the room and turn towards the stairs. I take them two at a time in my excitement to get started.

Ivy won't know what I'm doing or even think to ask any questions I'm not ready to answer yet if I do the research on the computer in my room. I chuckle to myself, feeling kind of like I'm trying to get away with something because I know she would be the first person to ask me what I was up to. Then again, if she feels at all like I do, this will be an incredible surprise for both of us.

"You're welcome," dad calls after me. I chuckle as I walk into my room, eager for what I might be able to find.

Chapter 18

Max

Mom, dad and I sit down at the simple, but beautifully decorated table. The tablecloth is cream and painted with red Poinsettias of all different sizes. The apple green napkins and darker green napkin rings enhance the green leaves of the flowers. The long five tiered black metal candelabra sits low in the middle of the table, with five, short, ivory pillar candles embedded with red flowers, enriched by their greens. My dad lights them, per Ivy's request and then returns to his seat.

Since I moved back home, I don't like to dress up very often. In Manhattan I had to wear a suit every single day for work, so now I like to look nice and still be comfortable when I can. Just like I did for the Christmas party, I'm dressed in nice jeans, with a deep blue ribbed sweatshirt, with a brown button at my neck. At least now that I'm older, my mom lets that kind of thing slide as long as she thinks I look "nice". My dad of course dresses up a little more for my mom, with a light blue button down, light gray pants and a navy patterned tie. I glance at my mom and can't help but notice how anxious she looks just sitting and waiting to be served at her own table. She's wearing an ivory, lacy, short sleeve top, with a red, green and gold, silk scarf tied at her neck. Her olive green pants match her scarf perfectly, like always. She continues to fidget and I fight to hold back my grin, while she impatiently waits for Christmas Eve dinner to start.

"Ivy, can I help you with anything?" she finally calls out towards the kitchen. I press my lips tightly together, attempting to hold back my chuckle.

Just then Ivy enters the dining room, carrying two of our white Christmas plates filled with food. I recognize the plates from the ivy and mistletoe painted around the edges. I grin, wishing I could get Ivy under the mistletoe again, but this time without any annoyances. She looks absolutely gorgeous in black dress pants and a simple blush short sleeve top that seems to flow around her. It comes down in a v in the front with the left side layering over the right and flaring at the waist. She has her hair pulled up in a basic ponytail, but even that doesn't look simple on her, with loose curls falling out on both sides of her face. "No, thank you. I've got it," she responds, politely, to my mom. "It's the least I can do," she emphasizes, as if she owes us for having her here, but we all know that's the furthest thing from the truth.

She sets a plate down in front of my dad, before setting the second plate down in front of me, with a sweet smile. We both mumble our appreciation, "Thank you." I take a deep breath and close my eyes, enjoying the delicious scent of the food she made in the air. I open my eyes just as she returns with two more plates, one for my mom and the last one for herself.

"Ivy, this looks amazing," dad praises. She places her plate on the table as she takes a seat across from me, joining us at the table. She scoots her chair in and glances up at my dad with a grateful smile.

"It certainly does," mom agrees.

"Thank you," Ivy grins.

I glance down at my plate and question, "What is it?" It smells incredible, but I have no idea what I'm looking at. It looks like some kind of roll stuffed with something, some potatoes and a vegetable mixture with both green and red accents.

She looks across the table and explains politely, as if we're at a restaurant, causing the corners of my mouth

162

to twitch up in amusement. "For our Christmas Eve dinner, I have prepared Beef Wellington with a mushroom duxelle, duchess potatoes and charred Brussels sprouts, with cranberries in a balsamic glaze," she announces, proudly. "Please, enjoy," she encourages as she looks around nervously at all three of us.

My mom's mouth drops open in surprise. "You made this in my kitchen?" she prompts, her admiration evident.

Ivy blushes a beautiful shade of pink and nods in confirmation, smiling shyly. "Yes, of course," she concurs, with a shrug as if it were no big deal.

"I didn't buy Wellingtons," mom declares, still somewhat puzzled.

Ivy shrugs again, "I know. I had extra pastry dough from the spinach artichoke bombs, so I made this instead of the steak and mushrooms you were going to make."

"Wow," dad expresses, with amazement.

I stare at my plate in complete shock at her admission. My eyes widen in wonder, as I take in the beautiful display and mouth-watering smelling food. Even my mom has never done anything like this, at least not that I recall and I feel like this is something I'd remember. Where did this girl come from?

"Max, is that okay?" Ivy whispers, sounding apprehensive.

I glance up at her and then look back down at my plate in complete awe. Everything not only looks delicious, it appears absolutely perfect. I focus back on her and mumble, "I just don't know what to say."

Dad chuckles and his eyes light up in amusement. "That's a first, Ivy. You actually rendered my son speechless," he proclaims and grins, mischievously.

I grimace, "Oh, Dad." I pretend to laugh along with him, before quickly snapping my mouth shut. I narrow my eyes at him, hoping he understands my not so subtle look of warning. He offers me a shrug, as if to say he knows he's right.

"Well, dig in," Ivy encourages, again.

I reach my hands out to both my mom and my dad, while they do the same with both Ivy and me. We all join hands. Then, as a gentle reminder, dad softly announces, "First we say Grace."

"Oh, of course," Ivy mumbles, her cheeks slightly pink. Then, she clasps both of my parents' outstretched hands.

We bow our heads and close our eyes while we wait for dad to begin. "Lord, thank you for this delicious meal we are about to eat. Thank you for keeping us safe in the storm. Please watch over us, and all of our friends and family, especially Ivy's family, who is missing their beloved girl this year." I open my eyes and glance across the table towards Ivy. It has to be incredibly hard on her and her family, not being able to be together for Christmas, but she seems to take it all in stride. The more I get to know her, the more she amazes me. I force myself to tear my gaze away from her and close my eyes as my dad continues the prayer. I don't want to get caught staring at her. I peek up at her one more time and grin. Maybe I do want her to catch me looking. "Thank you for bringing Ivy into our lives and for all the blessings you bestow upon us. In your name we pray. Amen," he declares.

"Amen," we all echo, before releasing each other's hands.

"Bon appetit!" mom offers, with a broad smile. She lays her napkin in her lap and picks up her fork, ready to start eating.

I reach for my own fork and knife, instantly digging in. "Mm," I groan in appreciation, at the same time as my dad. I immediately cut another bite as I chew.

I don't even pay attention to my mom and dad's conversation with Ivy. I can't do anything but focus on my food. My mouth waters as I savor the flavors of every single bite. "I usually don't like Brussels sprouts, but these are so good," I admit, appreciatively. Then, I pop another one into my mouth. I keep eating, until my plate is completely empty and I'm so full, I feel as if I'm about to burst. I finally set my fork down with a satisfied groan and I pat my stomach in satisfaction. I tap the table three times with the palm of my hand and notice the questioning look Ivy throws my way, as if she's waiting for me to say something. "That's it. I tap out," I announce.

Her eyebrows draw down further in confusion. I grin, realizing she doesn't understand what I'm talking about. Dad quickly jumps in and explains, "It's a wrestling reference."

Ivy's eyes instantly snap to mine, wide with curiosity. "You're a wrestler?" she prods, with obvious interest.

I huff a laugh and admit, "Not anymore."

"He was great," dad brags.

Mom sits up a little straighter and squares her shoulders. Then she proudly announces, "Pennsylvania state champion two years in a row."

Ivy's eyes widen even further in surprise. "Really?" she questions, a small smile playing on her lips.

I chuckle and remind her, "Don't be so surprised, Princess. There's a lot you don't know about me."

She blushes again, causing my stomach to churn at her beauty. She smiles and acknowledges, "I'm sure, but I just couldn't picture you as a wrestler."

My eyes widen and my heart drops anxiously into my stomach, as I notice my mom shifting in her seat out of the corner of my eye. I know exactly what she's thinking. I turn to her and give her the best warning look I'm able to muster. "Oh, no, Mom! Don't," I demand, attempting to stop her before she even suggests it.

She grins in amusement at my reaction and turns to Ivy without acknowledging me at all. "Let's leave the boys to cleanup," she suggests. "I'll show you some pictures of Max from high school," she announces, gleefully.

I groan inwardly and feel my face heat. "Mom, that's like ten years ago," I complain. "Don't show those photos," I plead. I'm sure she would show her much more than just a few wrestling photos from high school, no matter what she claims right now.

Ivy smiles over at me, her look mischievous, before she focuses on my dad. "Charles, if you and Max don't mind cleaning up, I would love to see these pictures," she emphasizes, her expression one of complete delight.

"I mind," I declare, pointing a finger back at myself for emphasis. I don't need my mom showing Ivy any old pictures of me.

"Well, I don't," dad responds, smirking. "Come on, Max," he insists. I groan again before I reluctantly push back from the table and stand up. I pause to watch as Ivy walks over and sits on the tan couch in the sitting area and our small white dog, ColeCole jumps up and climbs right into her lap, making me smile. Of course she adores her. Ivy begins petting her, while she waits for my mom. I sigh in defeat and pick up my plate and silverware. I trudge around the table, collecting what I'm able to carry, before striding towards the kitchen, with my arms full of dishes.

We quickly clear the table, but before we begin washing the dishes, I remember the promise I made to Ivy earlier about doing her family's wish tradition after dinner tonight. I smile as I think about the way she looked at me when I declared that it would be a date. "Hey, Dad," I call, to get his attention.

He looks over at me and inquires, "Yes, Max?"

"Remember Ivy's wish tradition we were talking about this morning?" I question, to jog his memory.

He nods slowly in confirmation, "Yes."

"Well, we said we were going to do that tonight after dinner," I remind him. "How about we get all of that set up for her, before we finish the dishes," I suggest.

"You're not just trying to put off doing the dishes, are you?" he challenges, with an arch of his eyebrow.

I laugh. Then I arch my eyebrows, mirroring him and point at myself in disbelief. "Who, me?" I question with mock innocence.

He chuckles and gives a slight shake of his head. He knows I'll put dishes or any type of cleaning off as long as I can, but I really do want to do this for Ivy too. In my book, that's a win-win for everyone. "Max," he murmurs my name in amusement.

I grin and ask, "What do you think, Dad?"

He nods in agreement, "Sure."

"Great!" I exclaim, excited to do this for her. "Can you get some Christmas mugs and make the hot chocolate?" I request.

"What are you going to do?" he challenges me.

"I'll grab some pens and cut strips of paper. Plus, I'll set it up in front of the fire place so it's comfortable and it looks festive and special too," I inform him.

He nods in agreement, "Okay."

I walk over to the drawer to the right of the refrigerator and grab a piece of paper and four pens. I swiftly cut the paper into four long strips, all about the same size, before I head to the living room. I glance at the coffee table and an idea suddenly pops into my head. I smile to myself and quickly stride for the garage, remembering the shelves with bins of unused Christmas decorations. I whistle a Christmas tune in my head as I get to work. I'm thrilled I'm able to do something for Ivy to help make her feel even just a little bit closer to home.

Chapter 19

Ivy

I smile to myself as I pet ColeCole, sitting quietly in my lap. The repetitive motion helps sooth my emotions. I feel like my heart is bouncing all around inside my chest since I met Max. Every minute I spend with him, I think I like him more and more. I can't believe Max used to wrestle and it sounds like he was really good. I shouldn't be surprised, but I guess I get excited every time I learn anything new about him. I imagine he was a good-looking kid, with how gorgeous of a man he's grown up to be now. My heart jumps up to my throat and I feel my face heat at my errant thoughts. I continue petting the dog in my lap, attempting to calm down my racing heart.

Judy rounds the back of the couch and sits down next to me with a large scrapbook in her hands. She happily announces, "Here it is."

I grin broadly at the picture of a very young Max peeking through the front cover of the light blue and white 12 x 12 scrapbook. "What is this?" I question, eager to find out more about him and see the pictures of him inside.

Judy grins and opens up the photo book. She quickly flips to the middle of the book, until she finds exactly what she's looking for. "This is mostly photos of Max from his senior year of high school but if you want to flip back after, there are also a few photos from when he was even younger," she advises.

The first picture she points out is one of his school pictures from high school. I smile down at the photo. His green eyes are incredibly bright and his smile completely contagious. "Oh my goodness, he looks so young," I murmur, feeling giddy. I can't help but add to myself that I was right. He really was a handsome kid. I bite my lower lip, admiring the photo.

"Well, he was seventeen when this picture was taken," she notifies me.

"So cute," I mumble, softly.

She grins over at me. I feel my face heat, the moment I realize I just said that out loud. "I like to think he's still cute. Don't you?" she challenges.

I feel my face turn an even deeper shade of red, while I giggle uncomfortably under her gaze. "Nice try, Judy," I mumble, awkwardly.

Her eyes widen, feigning innocence. "I'm not trying anything," she insists. "A woman can always appreciate a man's good looks, can't she?" she urges.

I take a deep breath and let it out slowly. I focus back on the scrapbook, not wanting to look at her as I answer her question, honestly this time. "Yes," I confirm, "Max is very handsome," I admit, feeling shy and a little overwhelmed. My heartbeat speeds up again, just saying those words aloud.

I feel her eyes on me for a moment as I look at the pictures. I try to pretend I don't notice, but I usually wear my emotions on the outside. She finally breaks the silence and reveals, "He thinks you're very pretty too."

I gasp in surprise. My head quickly snaps up to look at her and I meet her smiling eyes. "He said something?" I question, eagerly. My stomach churns with nervous energy and my heart pounds erratically as I wait for her response.

"No," she laughs, softly. "I'm his mother," she says, as if I may have forgotten. "I can tell," she claims, assessing me for my reaction.

I slowly release the breath I didn't know I was holding and shake my head in amusement. "You and my mother would really get along," I mumble. They really are so much alike. It almost makes it feel like I'm already home...almost.

I try not to think about what Max might think of me and instead focus on the pictures of him. I come across a very young picture of him and another boy who looks a lot like him, both wearing medals around their necks. "That's Max and his cousin. That was one of Max's first wrestling tournaments. He was so proud of winning that medal...the first of many," she murmurs, obviously lost in her own memories.

I turn the page and laugh at the image of an older Max wearing a red Junior Olympics zip up sweatshirt with an American flag on the sleeve. He has his sweatshirt unzipped partway to reveal another medal around his neck, but this time there's not even a hint of a smile on his face. "He must either be exhausted or didn't want his picture taken," I grin, pointing towards the picture. I have to admit that he still looks really cute, even without his beautiful smile, but I'm not about to say that out loud, especially to his mom.

Judy laughs along with me and nods her head, "I think it might've been a little of both, if I remember correctly." I turn to the next page and she points to the picture of Max with his hair styled perfectly, dressed incredibly in a black tuxedo with a red tie, and his brilliant smile that makes my insides melt. The older he gets in the pictures, the more he looks like himself and the more he makes my heart full. "That's a picture of Max getting ready for Prom," she informs me.

I nod my head in acknowledgement. He looks incredible all dressed up, but I feel a sudden twist of jealousy take root in my stomach at the thought of him dancing with someone else. My absurd reaction causes me to pinch my lips tightly together, so I don't say

171

anything about it. I didn't even know him then. Besides the fact that I don't even know if Max likes me now. I bite my bottom lip and attempt to push my irrational feelings aside.

I flip back towards the beginning of the scrapbook, to see some of the pictures I missed. I smile at the adorable photos of Max as a baby, then one of him as a toddler in a karate uniform. I turn the page to find a few middle school pictures, immediately noticing the charming curl of his hair. I come across a few more family photos, before I return to the high school pictures we started with. The ones where he begins to look more like the Max I've come to know and enjoy being around; the Max that makes my heart race just by walking into the room; the Max I wish would be mine.

"Have you ever thought that maybe Max is your reason?" Judy suddenly suggests, distracting me from my thoughts, as well as the album in my lap.

I look up at her curiously and question, "What do you mean?" She can't mean what it sounds like, can she?

She purses her lips thoughtfully, before responding. "Well, everything happens for a reason," she begins, repeating the same words she said to me the night I arrived. "Maybe your reason for getting stuck in Bethlehem was to meet Max," she intimates, as she studies me closely for my reaction.

I shake my head, instantly anxious. I begin turning the pages of the album without actually seeing anything. "I...I don't know, Judy," I stammer.

"But it is a possibility," she prods, pointedly. "Don't you think?" she questions, pushing me for an answer.

I close the photo album and glance towards the kitchen, thinking about everything that has happened the last few days. I may not understand it, but I feel a strong

172

pull towards Max. We may have had a little bit of a rough start, but things smoothed out pretty swiftly. I want to spend time with him and find out everything I can about him. He has taken over my dreams and I look forward to seeing him and talking to him the moment I wake up. He definitely makes my heart do crazy things inside my chest every time I look at him or even just think about him. What if he is my reason? But even if he is, can I admit to his mom that he might be my reason? I glance at her out of the corner of my eye and then return my gaze to my lap. I take a deep breath and exhale slowly. I gulp down the lump in my throat and without looking up at her; I shrug my shoulders and casually concede, "Anything is possible, I guess."

Judy sits a little bit taller, but gratefully she doesn't push me any further regarding Max. Instead, she requests, "Just promise me that you will stay in touch once you leave." My heart clenches tightly at the reminder of leaving here, especially at the thought of leaving Max. I'm excited to go home, but I can at least admit to myself that I'm going to miss him when I go. I'll miss all of them, but Max...I just don't want it to be the end of our story when I have to leave.

I nod and meet her gaze, as I smile at her in agreement. "Of course, I will," I maintain. "This is a Christmas that I will never, ever forget," I emphasize. For more reasons than I'm willing to admit out loud at the moment.

She grins back at me and concurs, "Neither will I." Her affirmation causes my heart to swell even more for this family. It's really not just Max I'm going to miss!

I need a change in subject, away from leaving and away from Max. I immediately think about everything this family has done for my self-confidence when it comes to my food and cooking for other people, especially Judy.

"You know the way that everyone has appreciated my cooking…" I begin and pause, waiting for her nod of acknowledgement. "It has really inspired me to take a bigger step," I inform her.

"Oh?" she prods, curiously.

I nod my head in confirmation. "Yeah," I mumble. "I've always dreamed of having a restaurant, but I never thought I could do it," I admit, sheepishly.

"Really?" she questions, obviously taken aback by my hesitation. "You single-handedly cooked for nearly two hundred people yesterday!" she reminds me; as if it were something I could forget.

I gasp and my eyes widen in disbelief at the number. I immediately clarify, "It wasn't that many people, was it?"

She nods and exclaims, "It had to be! The entire town was invited and I think everyone made it here, despite the storm."

I shake my head, shocked at what I was able to help Judy pull off. "Well, that's what I mean. And then tonight, it was like I was doing a chef's table. It was a really amazing feeling," I declare, proudly and give her a broad smile.

"You're terrific at what you do," she compliments me, sincerely.

I smile, grateful, but it almost immediately turns into a grimace, as I think about the other side of owning a restaurant. "The problem is that I only cook," I reveal, attempting to justify my hesitation. "I wouldn't know the first thing about the business side of things," I explain. Just because I love working in the kitchen and sharing my food with people, doesn't mean I know what to do when it comes to all the other parts of the restaurant business.

Judy shrugs like the business end of owning a restaurant is an easy obstacle to overcome, but I can't even imagine what it would take. "Max could help you with that," she suggests.

My mouth drops open and my eyes widen in obvious surprise. "Max?" I question, with a touch of disbelief in my tone.

"Sure," she confirms. "He has a Masters in business. He was on track to be a CFO before he moved back here," she enlightens me.

"Max?" I repeat, astonished. I remember when she told me he was working for a big company in Manhattan before he moved back home. I also remember he has a degree from an Ivy league school, but no one ever told me what he was really doing before he started working for his dad to help his family. "Your son, Max?" I question again, needing clarification.

She grimaces faintly, making me blush. She reminds me, "I told you, Ivy. He left his job to come home and help with the family."

I nod in agreement, "Yes, but you never said what he did." I pause before asking, "Why didn't he ever go back?

She sighs and purses her lips, thinking for a moment, before she answers me. "I don't know," she answers, with a shrug of her shoulders. "I honestly never asked. He knows he can leave if he wants to," she states. She tilts her head to the side and assesses me carefully, before claiming, "I think he was waiting for you."

I feel my cheeks heat and my stomach flip-flops. I can't believe Max's mom just said that to me. I look down at the closed album in my lap, not able to stop myself from wondering if it could possibly be true. Do I have a chance at a future with Max?

"Mom!" Max yells to her from the other room, disrupting my train of thought, as well as our conversation.

"Yes?" she calls back.

"Can you bring Ivy into the living room for a minute?" he requests.

She glances at me and both of our eyes instantly fill with curiosity. Then she informs him, "We'll be right there."

My heart beats a little faster as I speculate what he has up his sleeve now. We both stand up and I set the photo album down on the coffee table. We walk towards the living room, and I hear the jingling of ColeCole's collar, as he jumps down off the couch and chases after us.

Chapter 20

Max

I stride into the family room carrying two tall Christmas mugs filled with hot chocolate. I place them on the coffee table, on top of the green painted Christmas tray. One mug is red with snow and stockings and the other one is green with ornaments decorating the sides. Dad does the same as me, placing his mugs on the opposite side of the table on top of the red painted Christmas tray. "This looks really good, Max," dad compliments me, as he takes a seat on the floor.

"Thank you," I respond simply. I glance at the rustic tiled fireplace behind us with a boy and girl elf on each side, similar to the ones standing by our front door. I turn my head to peak at the Christmas tree, making sure all the lights are on. Then, I glance back at the table to make sure everything is in place. I covered the coffee table with one of our red Christmas tablecloths and put down the two trays, painted with simple Christmas items, including a snowman, candy canes, stockings, Santa and a reindeer. I placed a large white poinsettia with a touch of gold along the edges, but without the stem or even a pot on each tray. I filled a large, red, oval, Christmas platter with a variety of Christmas cookies we had hidden away before the Christmas party, so we didn't have to do any more baking after the party. Of course, it includes some of the cookies Ivy made, but I did help. I put the pens and strips of paper next to the tray closest to me, so I have them within reach while I'm sitting down. I straighten my legs out in front of me and cross them at the ankles, before I lean back on my hands and ask for my mom and Ivy to come in. "I guess we're ready," I announce, with a glance at my dad. He nods in agreement as he readjusts his seat on the floor.

I take a deep breath and exhale slowly, just before I call for them. I don't know why I'm feeling a little nervous, but I definitely am. My heart begins to palpitate and butterflies take over my stomach as we wait for them to step into the room. My breath catches the moment I see Ivy round the corner, but I force myself to take another breath. "You can't possibly be done with the dishes already," Ivy teases.

I grin up at her, loving the look of awe that covers her face the moment she takes everything in. "Nope," I declare. The corners of my mouth twitch up, while a feeling of complete satisfaction washes over me, as her eyes light up with pure joy.

I hand Ivy a mug as she approaches me, while my dad hands one to my mom. "What's all this?" mom inquires, sounding surprised.

"We thought we could do Ivy's wish tradition," dad happily announces. I smile at Ivy. Then, I watch in awe, as her face softens even more than I thought possible, as she registers that we did all of this for her. My heart skips a beat in response.

Ivy sits down on the floor next to me, tucking her feet underneath her, while my mom lowers herself to the floor, sitting between her and my dad. "What a great idea," mom praises. Then, she gives a nod of approval in my direction.

I reach for the papers and pens and hand them out to everyone. Then, I smile again at Ivy, my heart beginning to pound. "So, tell us what to do, Princess," I advise.

She grins up at me so brightly, that she causes my breath to get stuck in my throat. "Okay," she happily agrees. "It's simple, really. Just write what your deepest wish for Christmas is, then fold the paper in half," she instructs.

"That's it?" I question.

"That's the first step," she concurs.

We all take a moment to think about what we want to write. It doesn't take me long at all. I know exactly what I want. I grin as I write down my wish and fold my paper in half. Then, I look up at her and prompt, "Now what?"

She pushes up and leans over towards the fireplace as she tells us what to do. "Now, you place it right in front of the fire place, as close to the fire as you can without burning it," she explains. "Like this," she directs. Then, she demonstrates, carefully placing her paper right at the edge of the fireplace. I follow her movements and do the same with my paper, situating it next to hers. Then, my mom, followed by my dad, both do the same thing on the other side of the fireplace.

"What's next?" I request.

She settles back in and picks up her hot chocolate, cradling it in her hands. "Well, we sip hot chocolate and maybe eat a few cookies," she replies, her eyes sparkling.

"I like that part," I mumble. She laughs, causing her whole face to light up. I take a sip of hot chocolate, hoping to gulp down the sudden lump in my throat.

"And we hope our wishes disappear up the chimney and make their way into Santa's sleigh," she finishes with a broad grin. Then, I watch as she takes a sip of her hot cocoa.

"Really?" I probe. I can't help but feel slightly disappointed there isn't a little more something to it. I want to spend as much time as I can with her. I thought doing this tradition with her would be a wonderful reason to keep her here next to me for a while, but this is over way too fast.

"Yes," she confirms. "Sometimes they go and sometimes they don't. That's the fun of it," she discloses and shrugs her shoulders.

"You have a strange sense of fun, Princess," I tease her, barely able to fight back my own smile.

"Max!" mom warns, assuming I'm being rude again.

Ivy just shrugs it off, making me feel as if she already understands me better. "It's okay," she tells my mom. "I know it's silly," she grins sheepishly. I couldn't stop myself from smiling back at her, even if Christmas depended on it. "My last wish came true senior year of college," she enlightens us, piquing my curiosity.

"What was your wish?" I inquire.

She glances at me nervously and then she reveals, "I wished that I would get into culinary school in Charleston."

My eyes widen in surprise. "That's a wasted wish, if you ask me," I state. I think she could get into any culinary school in the world with her talent.

"She didn't ask you," dad scolds me, but I don't' bother explaining why I made that statement. I want to hear her explanation.

"It's fine," Ivy instantly waves off my comment, hopefully understanding my meaning. "It may seem silly, but I was really happy with everything with my life. I wanted to go to culinary school in Charleston, but it was super expensive," she emphasizes. "Then, the day after Christmas, I found out I got a full ride," she explains, a proud smile lighting up her face.

"Really?" I prod, my own heart filling with pride. Knowing Ivy earned such an amazing scholarship doesn't really surprise me. She's incredibly talented and if they tasted any of her cooking, they were probably begging her to come to their school.

She nods in confirmation and mumbles, "Yeah." Then, she shrugs and adds, "Call it what you want, but my Christmas wish was granted."

I nod my head in understanding, but another question comes to my mind. "But why make a wish on Christmas Eve?" I ask, curiously. "Don't people usually make wishes on their own birthdays when they blow out their candles, or something?"

"Sure," she nods, "but the magic of Christmas helps make wishes come true," she proclaims, with absolute certainty.

Mom smiles at Ivy, obviously adoring her answer. In fact, it sounds like something my mom might say. She declares, "I think that's wonderful, Ivy."

"Thank you, Judy," she murmurs appreciatively in response. "And if I ever get married and have kids, I want to pass this tradition on to them," she announces her cheeks tinting pink.

My stomach twists at the thought of Ivy getting married and having kids with someone else. I almost can't believe I'm thinking this, but I don't want that to happen. We need to spend more time together to figure out if we have a future together. But the thought of Ivy having her life go in a direction away from me and towards someone else, anyone else, honestly makes it difficult to breathe.

"That's sweet," mom praises.

"Thank you," Ivy replies. I'm grateful when Ivy lightens the mood a little bit. She smirks and adds, "And it's a great way to see what your kids really want for Christmas." We all laugh in response. Even though you wouldn't know their wish until the last minute, it's definitely true.

"So what's the plan for tomorrow?" I ask everyone, but keep my focus on Ivy. I already know what our family plan usually is for Christmas Day. I want to hear what she thinks.

"If it's okay with you, I'd like to sleep in," she requests.

"Absolutely," mom instantly agrees. "You deserve it," she emphasizes.

She's right, Ivy definitely deserves it, but I can't stop myself from teasing her anyway. I attempt to keep a straight face as I gasp and then I ask her with mock despair, "What no breakfast?"

Ivy gives me a look and playfully pushes my arm, when she realizes I'm joking. I fall to the side in exaggeration, before righting myself and bumping lightly back into her. "There's cereal in the pantry!" Ivy suggests, laughing. Mom joins in the laughter, amused with our banter.

When Ivy stops and catches her breath, she covers her mouth, unsuccessfully attempting to hide her yawn. "You're tired," I mumble, stating the obvious.

She gives me a small, but content smile, making my heartbeat race at the sleepy look on her face. "If you don't mind, I'd like to go to bed a little early tonight. I'm still worn out from yesterday," she admits, reluctantly.

I grin mischievously and nod my head. "Yeah. You don't want to fall asleep on the couch again," I volunteer. I want to remind her how I carried her up to her room last night after she fell asleep on the couch, while I was talking to her. I still can't believe she slept through my whole confession, but I made sure to take good care of her. She blushes a beautiful shade of pink, causing my smile to broaden.

"You go ahead, Ivy," mom insists.

She leans over and gives my mom a hug before she stands up. "Thank you for everything, Judy," she reiterates, sincerely.

"You're welcome," she grins. "Merry Christmas, Ivy," she proclaims.

"Merry Christmas," Ivy repeats. Then, she carefully steps around me, before she suddenly stops, as something else comes to her mind. "Oh!" she exclaims. She spins back around towards us to give us one more direction. "And no reading anyone else's wishes," she instructs. "You can't even check whose wish goes up the chimney until Christmas morning. It's bad luck," she warns, giving me a hard stare. Then, she smirks down at me and adds teasingly, "For eight years." I laugh softly as she winks playfully at me, causing my heart to skip a beat.

"Good night, Princess," I murmur, softly. I'm not able to wipe the smile off my face as I look up at her.

"Good night, Ivy," dad says.

"Good night," she replies, her eyes still focused on me. Then, she finally turns, breaking our gaze. I watch her until she disappears up the stairs.

"I really like her," dad admits.

"So do I," mom agrees.

I continue staring in the direction she just disappeared, with a smile on my face. Without thinking, I quietly disclose, "Yeah, I like her, too."

"I knew it!" mom exclaims, her excitement palpable.

She instantly garners my attention with her outburst, snapping me out of my Ivy induced daze. "Mom," I groan her name in warning, with the smile finally wiped off my face. I turn away from her and reach for a Gingerbread cookie. I take a bite of the cookie and attempt to ignore my mom's intense focus on me. She's smiling brightly at me, her expression completely hopeful. I don't want to encourage her, but just thinking about Ivy brings a smile back to my face. Even my mom's incessant need to interfere with my love life, isn't about to ruin my mood. Ironically I might even be on the same page as my mom for once, at least when it comes to Ivy.

"You did a good thing tonight, Max," mom vehemently proclaims.

"Yes, you did," dad agrees.

I nod in acknowledgement, but I'm suddenly hit with a tightness in my chest. Tonight was nice, but how do I make Christmas morning good for her? I feel myself beginning to panic. She's still going to wake up here on Christmas morning, instead of being home with her family. We don't even have any presents for her. How can you wake up on Christmas morning without having anything to open? I have to do something for her!

"Are you okay?" mom inquires. I glance at her. She's looking at me with her eyebrows drawn down in concern, instantly reading my change in mood.

I gulp and stiffly nod my head in confirmation. "Yeah, I'm fine, but would you and dad mind cleaning-up?" I request.

"We didn't even finish the dishes from dinner," dad reminds me.

I nod my head, "I know. I'll make it up to you. I promise. I just remembered I have something I have to take care of before tomorrow morning and I'm not sure how long it will take," I concede.

Mom and dad look at each other with wide eyes, obviously wanting to ask more questions. Mom opens her mouth, but dad covers her hand with his and gives her a look to stop her from pushing the issue. It appears as if they have a silent conversation. Then, dad turns back to me and quickly speaks up. "Don't worry about it, Max. We can finish cleaning everything up tonight," he insists. Mom gives him another look, with a hint of a smile and he quickly rephrases his statement. "I'll finish everything up tonight," he announces.

Mom grins and offers, "I'll help you, Charles."

I quickly jump up to leave before they change their minds. "Thanks, Mom," I proclaim and kiss her on the top of the head. "Thanks, Dad," I add, giving him an appreciative smile. I turn and quickly stride for the stairs, hoping I'm able to easily come up with a wonderful idea for Ivy, without any time left to do it.

Chapter 21

Max

I sit in the high-back chair at my long, curved, black desk in the corner of my bedroom, opposite my Queen sized bed and stare at my computer screen, everything starting to blur together. I heave a heavy sigh as I scroll through various kitchen tools and gadgets, trying to find the perfect Christmas present for Ivy. I rub my eyes, tired from staring at the computer for so long. I close my eyes and stretch out my neck and back, my whole body beginning to feel tense from sitting in the same position this whole time. I sigh again and open my eyes.

I stare at my sage green walls for a moment trying to gather my thoughts. Looking for a present like this seems pointless. Especially when I know it will be impossible to get her anything like this in time for her to open it on Christmas morning. I drop my hands to my desk and scowl in frustration. It feels completely unattainable knowing I only have a few hours left to have something incredible for her under the Christmas tree, not even a few days. I really want her to have something extraordinary, which makes this even more difficult. I just have no idea how to make it happen.

I groan and refocus my attention on my computer screen, once again. I glare at the kitchen products website, almost like I'm blaming it for my problem and at the same time, begging it to give me the answer I need. Ivy deserves to have something special to open on Christmas morning, especially since she can't be with her family. I just have to keep trying, even if I don't sleep. I have to figure out something I can do. I just have no idea where to even look anymore. I grit my teeth and continue to scroll, hoping something will spark an idea.

"Good night, Max. Max? Max!" dad yells my name to get my attention, startling me in my seat. I instantly snap my head up and acknowledge him.

"Oh, hey Dad," I mutter. "Sorry," I apologize and heave a heavy sigh. "I guess I'm a little distracted," I confess, absentmindedly. Then, I immediately turn back towards the computer and continue scrolling. I don't have time to do anything else.

He chuckles as he looks over my shoulder at the computer screen. Then, he instantly questions, "What are you doing?"

"Research," I reply, without looking at him.

"On," he prompts, dragging out the word. He stares at me and remains quiet, waiting for my response.

I sigh again and lean back in my chair, so I can look up at him. I finally notice he's all ready for bed, wearing the same Christmas pajamas as me. I may have said I wasn't going to do it this year, but my mom talked me into it, again. I just can't seem to say, no to her, especially on Christmas. I never can and since she's my mom, I'm pretty sure she knows that about me. At least they're comfortable this year. Unfortunately, that's not always the case. This time the pants are a loose-fitting red and black flannel. The shirt has long black sleeves with red in the middle, reminding me of a baseball shirt. It has white writing on the front stating, "Have your ELF a Merry Christmas," with striped, stocking elf feet sticking down next to the word elf. Honestly, I think they're almost as crazy as Ivy's, but thankfully, not quite. She'd definitely still win that competition, I think to myself with a chuckle, as I recall her green, buttoned "no peeking" flap in the back of her PJ's.

I give myself a mental shake and focus on my dad's question. "I want to do something nice for Ivy," I enlighten him. "For Christmas," I add, clasping my hands in front of me. "You know?" I prod, anxiously.

Dad's eyes widen in surprise, although, he immediately nods his head in understanding. "Sure," he agrees.

I sigh in frustration, as I glance back at the computer screen, still having no clue what to do for her, and no direction on where to even look anymore. "I mean, she's away from her family for the first time for Christmas," I reiterate, trying to explain my reasoning. Then again, after our conversation at lunch earlier, he should know a lot of other reasons why I want to do something special for her, but maybe it will help to talk through it. "I know she had a great time at the party and dinner tonight was awesome," I declare, with a wide smile, "but part of her still has to be sad," I contemplate. My heart aches, wanting to help her. I've never had to spend a Christmas, or any holiday for that matter, away from my family. I can only imagine how hard it would be. Yet, Ivy already had to be alone for Thanksgiving and now here she is away from her family again, but this time for Christmas. Yet she's been nothing, but positive. Unless I was trying to annoy her, I smirk. I just want her to have a real reason to smile tomorrow morning and I want to be the one to give her something or do something to give her that reason.

He nods in agreement, "True."

"She cooked for the Christmas party and for tonight's dinner, which was...Wow," I announce, unsure how else to explain how phenomenal everything was. Especially since she just utilized the food we had in our house. I've never known someone who could be so creative in the kitchen. My mom is a great cook, but Ivy was able to come up with these fantastic dishes just by looking through the pantry and the refrigerator and seeing what kind of food we have in the house. "Don't you think I..." I trail off and momentarily pinch my lips tightly together. I take a deep breath and attempt to rephrase my question. "I mean, don't you think we," I emphasize, "should give her something really special for Christmas?" I prompt.

"Well, yes," he instantly agrees, without even a hint of hesitation. "Sure," he confirms, confident in his response.

"But what?" I question, with a little bit of the desperation I'm feeling. "I've been looking up kitchen tools and gadgets for over an hour and no one will be able to ship anything to get here for tomorrow morning!" I exclaim, stating the obvious.

"Well," dad begins.

I immediately interrupt, attempting to relay to him some of the things I've been thinking about. Maybe if I explain everything that I've considered, he can help me figure out a way to make something work. "I'm not making her something," I tell him, knowing that would be a disaster for everyone. I'm not exactly a creative person. "Mom's cooking dinner tomorrow," I state what we already know. I huff a laugh and declare, "I can barely make coffee, and so I'm definitely not even going to try to cook her breakfast."

"How about," he begins, trying again to give me a suggestion, but I still don't give him a chance to speak.

An idea pops into my head and I point to him, suddenly excited. "Oh!" I exclaim. I quickly blurt out my thoughts before I forget. "Maybe you can fix her car faster, so that she can get home sooner? Maybe even by Christmas dinner," I suggest. I'm sure she'd be thrilled to see her family anytime on Christmas. We just have to help get her there. "I know you're waiting on a part, but maybe we can find one in town on a junk car or something," I contemplate, talking out my idea aloud. I pause as a thought occurs to me. "That won't work," I grumble, irritably. I heave a sigh and shake my head at my own suggestion. "I don't want her to think I want to get rid of her." If I tried to rush her out of here, that's probably exactly what she would think. When in reality, that's actually the furthest thing from the truth.

"I have an idea," he announces, quickly, trying to get the words out before I interrupt him again.

I groan in frustration, already feeling defeated. I drop my head into my hands and cover my face with my hands. I run them over my face and then up through my hair, tugging lightly on the ends in irritation. I stare back at the computer screen, feeling completely hopeless. "I've had a lot of ideas, Dad," I whine. "This is absolutely impossible," I complain, irritably. I just wish I had thought to do something sooner. Even if I did this yesterday, I could've done overnight shipping and been able to get it in time, but of course I think of it hours before Christmas morning. "I've never wanted to do something nice for someone so badly before. It's making me crazy!" I stress. "I'm even looking up poems that I can write in a card or something, Dad. Poems!" I exclaim, exasperated. "Me!" I emphasize, with utter disbelief.

I drop my hands into my lap and turn to look at him to get his opinion, but he's no longer standing by my desk. "Dad?" I call, but he doesn't answer. He must've walked away while I was rambling on and on. I don't blame him, but this time I really could've used his help. I shrug my shoulders and heave another sigh as I turn and focus back on the computer screen, hoping for a better result. I grimace, feeling as if I'm just banging my head against the wall, instead of making any progress.

"Here," dad offers, as he steps back into my bedroom. He crosses the room in three long strides. He stands in front of me, with his hand outstretched and a look of determination on his face. He holds out a small folded strip of paper to me.

I look up at him and back down at the paper in his hand. I hesitantly take the paper from him as my eyebrows draw down in confusion. "What's this?" I question, cautiously.

"Ivy's wish," he enlightens me.

My eyes instantly widen in shock. "Dad!" I exclaim. I can't help but wonder if I should really look. My dad took Ivy's wish from the fireplace? A slow smile spreads across my face and I nod my head in agreement as I realize this is the perfect answer, at least I hope it will be. "Dad," I repeat, impressed with his thinking. "You dog, you," I tease him.

He shrugs and innocently asks, "What?"

I laugh at his reaction, suddenly feeling as if a weight has been lifted off my shoulders. I'm relieved to at least have somewhere to look for an idea. Hopefully, her wish will be something that's possible for me to make happen. Then, I give him a look of warning and tell him, "If I get eight years of bad luck for this..." I trail off, allowing my implication to hang in the air.

He grins and gives me a look, challenging me. Then he claims, "I think it might be quite the opposite, son."

I give him a grateful smile, knowing he could be right. Then, I hold my breath in anticipation, as I unfold the piece of paper. I quickly read Ivy's wish and fold it back up with resolve. I don't know why I didn't think about this way sooner.

"Well?" he questions.

I smile happily, finally satisfied with what to do for her, as long as I can get everything to fall into place. I nod my head in confirmation. This is absolutely perfect. I don't know how I didn't think of it. "I think I can do this," I proclaim. My mind begins racing, thinking about all the logistics to be able to make this happen immediately. I have to look something up before I do anything else.

"Yeah?" he prompts.

"Yeah," I confirm, confidently. I spin back towards my computer and begin typing in the search bar.

"Need help?" dad questions.

I look at the screen, thrilled with what I'm able to locate. A smile easily spreads across my face as I realize I'm already close to making this a reality. "No, I've got it," I confirm. I just need one more thing. I turn back towards my dad to stop him. "Actually, Dad, where's the phone that Ivy's been using to call home?" I question.

"In the kitchen," he informs me.

I nod in acknowledgement, feeling more hopeful by the minute. "Have you or mom used it today?" I probe.

Dad pauses to think about it before answering me. "I haven't," he verifies. "I don't think your mom has, either," he adds.

"Great!" I exclaim. I feel my excitement quickly building up inside of me. I jump up, pushing my chair back, letting it scrape across the wood floor. I clap my dad on the shoulder, grinning broadly. I happily announce, "You're the best, Pops!"

He chuckles softly and smiles back at me, as he follows me out of my room. I hurriedly stride for the kitchen, hoping to find the phone. "Good luck," he offers, with a small wave. Then, he turns towards his bedroom and opens the door.

"Thanks. I'll let you know what happens," I tell him, before he disappears inside. I know I might need more of his help, as well as my mom's, later on. But a few other things have to happen first, or this won't work at all. Most importantly, I need to talk to Ivy's family. Hopefully, they're able to help me with her present.

Chapter 22

Ivy

I sigh and roll over onto my back again. I can't sleep. I'm wide-awake and staring up at the white ceiling. My mind won't stop racing from one thing to the next. I can't believe it's Christmas Eve and I'm not home sleeping in my own bed. I miss my family and I wish I could wake up and see them in the morning, but I know that's impossible. Then again, when I think about being home for Christmas, I realize that if I were home, I wouldn't be spending Christmas with Max and his family. My heart already aches when I think about leaving here. I've grown to care about all of them so much, especially Max. I just wish I knew how he really felt about me.

I wonder what would've happened if I never tried to drive home for Christmas? I might've never even met Max and his family. The thought alone really makes me sad. I'm so grateful to Judy and Charles and even Max, for everything they've done for me. This whole family has not only made the last few days bearable, but absolutely wonderful. In fact, I don't think I could ever forget this Christmas and I owe that all to the Carson's.

A smile plays on my lips, as thoughts of Max cross through my mind. I giggle to myself, happily stunned that I've grown to like Max so much, but who could blame me? He's not at all who I thought he was when I first met him. Maybe we were both just tired and grumpy the night we met. Besides, even I can admit I was being a little bit stubborn about trying to drive home during a snowstorm, but I'm not about to tell him that. Some things are best kept to yourself and this is one of those things. He surprises me more and more every minute I spend with him, which causes me to want to spend as much time with him as possible. Ironically, Max is now the reason I'm actually a little thankful I'm still stranded here. I don't know what will happen when I have to leave and that really does scare me. When will I be able to see Max again? Will he even want to see me again? I sure hope so, but I have to stop dwelling on it.

My mind drifts to the wishes sitting downstairs near the fireplace, putting a smile on my face. I love how all of them made sure I still had some of the things that remind me of Christmas at home. Even if they seem like little things, they're huge for me. Max made everything look so festive for me too. It felt cozy and magical because of him. I wonder what he wished for? I wonder if any of the wishes are still there? Or maybe all of them are still there. I begin fidgeting and finally push myself out of bed, knowing I'm not about to fall asleep anytime soon, no matter how tired I am. I might as well wander downstairs to check if the wishes are all still there. "That couldn't hurt, right?" I mumble to myself.

I flip on the bedroom light and cautiously peek out into the hallway. I don't see any movement and I don't hear anying but silence. I slip out the door and quietly close it behind me before I tiptoe downstairs, the night lights my only guide. I noiselessly tiptoe through the foyer towards the living room. I immediately notice the fire has dimmed, with barely a few embers remaining. I vigilantly take one last look around before edging closer, noticing only three papers along the edge. I take one more step closer, when suddenly I hear a man clear his throat behind me, startling me.

I jump and gasp, as I spin around with my hand on my chest and my heart beating erratically. I'm met with Max's sparkling green eyes staring down at me. The corners of his lips twitch up in amusement. He stands in the entryway right under the mistletoe, with his arms crossed over his chest and his eyebrows arched in challenge. "Max!" I exclaim in a harsh whisper. "You almost gave me a heart attack!" I accuse him.

He grins, knowing exactly what he caught me doing, but he asks me anyway. "What are you doing, Princess?" he questions, his voice dripping with overt sweetness.

"Um, I...I...I..." I stammer, trying to come up with a good reason for why I'm wandering around downstairs. "I'm getting a glass of water," I finally blurt out. I emphatically nod my head, as if insisting it's the truth.

He smirks and points in the opposite direction of which I was headed. "The kitchen is that way," he reminds me.

I blush and nod my head. "Oh, right," I murmur. "I know. I thought I left my glass over there," I mumble, unconvincingly, as I point somewhere behind me.

He doesn't hold back his smile and barely hides his laughter, but at least he makes an effort not to laugh at me outright. Then, he informs me, "You're a terrible liar."

I blush a deeper shade of red and try to turn the tables on him. I square my shoulders and defiantly ask, "Well, what are you doing down here?"

"I was looking something up on the computer," he informs me. I pinch my lips tightly together. He's enjoying this way too much. His satisfaction at catching me attempting to peek at the wishes is more than evident.

I sigh in defeat, my shoulders sagging slightly. Then, I purse my lips and stare at him, wondering if he's really telling me the truth. "Mm, hmm," I reply, with a nod. "So whose wish is missing?" I probe, assessing his reaction.

He glances over at the fireplace, but doesn't move any closer, before he turns back to me. He shrugs and admits, "I don't know."

I grimace and try one more time. "You didn't check?" I prompt.

He shakes his head with a low chuckle. "No," he confirms, as if that would be a crazy thing to do. "You said it was bad luck for eight years if I did," he repeats my words from before.

At the reminder of eight years of bad luck, I give in. I bite my lower lip and glance up at the mistletoe above Max's head. I take a small step closer to him and release my lip. "I've heard of something else that can give you bad luck for eight years," I murmur, smiling shyly.

The corners of his mouth twitch up. "Yeah?" he questions, as if he doesn't know what I'm talking about. "What's that?" he prompts.

I look up at the mistletoe above his head. I wait until he follows my gaze and glances up, noticing the mistletoe. He smiles causing my heart to skip a beat. He looks down at me, as he drops his hands to his sides. I tilt my head to the side and glance up at him from underneath my eyelashes, a smile playing upon my lips. "Was this a setup?" I prod.

He laughs, the sound vibrating over me and giving me goosebumps. Then, he shakes his head in denial. "No, I swear," he insists, grinning broadly.

"Right," I tease him, playfully.

"Well, we wouldn't want eight years of bad luck," he reiterates. Then he takes a small step towards me, in an attempt to meet me in the middle. "Would we?" he challenges. He pauses and waits for my reaction.

I smile, while butterflies take over my insides. I clasp my hands behind my back and anxiously twist back and forth. I take a deep breath, trying to calm my nerves, as I attempt to answer innocently. "I know I wouldn't," I reveal, quietly.

"Neither do I," he whispers. My breath momentarily catches in my throat, as he stares into my eyes. He moves a little closer, his face instantly becoming serious, as he closes the distance between us. Then, he slowly leans down towards me. My heart begins racing. It's beating so hard and fast; it feels like it might jump right out of my chest. My breath quickens, matching his. I feel his warm breath on my lips and my eyes begin to flutter closed, hoping to feel his soft lips on mine. His hand reaches up and barely brushes my cheek.

The lights flicker on, startling us apart and shocking me back to reality. I blink rapidly, trying to get my bearings as Charles wanders down the stairs and into the room. I can't help but notice he's wearing the same pajamas Max currently has on, causing me to smile in amusement. Max glares at his dad, as he rounds the bottom of the stairs.

"Oh!" he exclaims the moment he sees both of us, unmoving, staring at him. "Hah!" he laughs, realizing where we're both standing. He grins broadly at the two of us and swiftly apologizes. "Sorry. I got a little hungry," he explains.

"Dad, I swear, you have the worst timing," Max grumbles. I bite my lip to hold back my own laughter.

"Ignore me," he insists. "I didn't see anything," he adds, with mock innocence. Then, he puts his hand up near his eyes to shield us from view as he walks in the direction of the kitchen.

I feel my face heat in embarrassment, wondering what he did actually see. "Well, that ruined the mood," Max mumbles.

I nod in agreement, feeling slightly uncomfortable. "Yeah, you could say that," I awkwardly agree.

"Charles?" Judy calls down the stairs in a harsh whisper. "Are you down here?" she questions, as quietly as she can when she's trying to yell downstairs.

Max drops his hands to his sides in annoyance. He loudly announces, "We're all down here, Mom!"

Judy strides down the stairs wearing the same pajamas as both Max and Charles. I burst out laughing, not able to hold it in. Max looks at me and arches his eyebrows in question. I attempt to reign in my laughter and quickly apologize, "I'm sorry." I catch my breath and explain, still grinning, "You guys really weren't kidding about the matching pajamas."

Max crosses his arms over his chest again and then he looks me up and down. I'm in the same Christmas pajamas he saw me in the first night, but his look only makes me giggle more. He rolls his eyes and turns back to his mom, as she steps up behind him. He sighs and informs her, "Dad's in the kitchen."

She starts towards the kitchen, when she suddenly stops and looks back and forth between the two of us, the corners of her mouth curving up. "What are you two doing down here?" she prompts, curiously.

"I was looking something up on the computer. I couldn't sleep," he informs her. His statement has me wondering where the computer is because I haven't seen it, but that doesn't mean it isn't around here somewhere.

"I needed a glass of water," I add, answering the question. I figure at this point I might as well stick with the story I told Max, even if he didn't believe me. At least it won't look like I'm trying too hard to make something up, like I did before.

"Let me get that for you," Max offers. I smile up at him, grateful. I watch as he walks away, heading towards the kitchen.

Judy stares intently at me, trying to hold back her smile. I can't help but feel anxious under her powerful scrutiny and begin fidgeting. I attempt to look away, but I feel her gaze on me. I grimace and clasp my hands tightly together to keep them still. I feel like I need to say something to defend myself, even though I haven't done anything. I look at her, feigning confidence. I give my head a firm shake and insist, "Nothing happened."

She shrugs her shoulders and her grin grows. "I didn't say anything," she claims, but I still feel her staring at me, as if she thinks she knows something.

"Judy, nothing happened," I emphasize.

She smiles even wider and gestures above my head. She appears almost giddy with excitement as she informs me, "You're standing under the mistletoe." I glance up at the mistletoe, that I already know is right above my head and take a deep breath. Then, I look back at her with wide eyes. She gleefully reminds me, "You don't want eight years of bad luck."

I sigh and shake my head in disbelief. "Not you too!" I complain.

"It's tradition," she proclaims, slightly defensive.

Max walks back into the room with a glass of water in his hand. "Here you go, Ivy," he offers, as he hands me the glass.

I take it and smile appreciatively up at him. "Thank you," I mumble. His mom continues to watch us in anticipation. I take a deep breath for courage. Then, I grip his arm for stability, warmth shooting through me the moment we touch. I push up on my tiptoes and softly place a kiss on Max's cheek. My lips already tingling from the contact, as I fall back on my heels. I glance anxiously up at him, hoping to see his reaction.

He smiles down at me, the look in his eyes causing my heart to skip a beat. "What was that for?" he prods, reverently.

I let go of his arm and offer him a timid smile, as I answer. "Mistletoe," I state, with mock confidence.

His grin broadens and I take a sip of my water to hide my own reaction to him. "Goodnight," I quietly mumble.

"Night," he whispers.

I walk up the stairs, slowly to maintain my balance, feeling his eyes on me the whole way. "Not one word," I hear him mutter a warning to his mom. I smile to myself, imagining the look Judy is giving to Max. Between the look she just gave me when she saw Max and me under the mistletoe and the things she does and says that remind me so much of my own mother, I think I know the exact way she's looking at him.

I slip into the bedroom and quietly close the door behind me. I put the glass of water down on the nightstand right next to the bed. Then I turn off the light and climb into bed, pulling the covers over me, as I lay down on my back. I smile to myself, no longer caring about the wishes on the fireplace. I close my eyes, my thoughts again consumed with Max. I can't help but wonder if he'll ever have the chance to kiss me. Maybe that should've been my wish. I giggle and curl up on my side. I close my eyes in hopes that this time, I'll be able to get some sleep.

Chapter 23

Ivy

I slowly open my eyes and stretch, attempting to wake myself up. I look around the room I've called mine the last few days and I suddenly realize what day it is today. I smile and joyfully whisper to myself, "It's Christmas." I may not be home, but I'm happy to be here. I'm grateful I met the Carson family, especially Max, I admit. I feel my face heat the instant he enters my thoughts. It feels like I go to sleep thinking of him and now I wake up the same way. As for family, I'll still get to spend Christmas with them. It just won't be on Christmas Day this year and I'm truly okay with that.

I climb out of bed, feeling energized. I pull my hair up into a messy bun on top of my head as I wander into the bathroom. I quickly brush my teeth and then I make my way downstairs. I walk into the kitchen, hoping Max is awake. I smile at Judy and Charles standing near the counter in their matching Christmas pajamas, quietly whispering to one another. "Merry Christmas," I greet them, cheerily.

Judy spins around and faces me. "Merry Christmas, Ivy!" she replies, gleefully.

At the same time, Charles proclaims, "Merry Christmas!"

I look around anxiously, but I don't see any sign of Max. My heart sinks, but I try to stay positive. "Max isn't awake yet?" I question. I was hoping he was like me and liked to wake up a little early on Christmas morning.

Judy shakes her head. "I haven't seen him this morning," she states.

"Neither have I," Charles adds.

Judy quickly jumps in to defend him. "He's been working so many hours lately. I don't blame him for sleeping in," she justifies.

I shake my head, trying to hide my disappointment because I know she's right. "Neither do I," I concede. I remind myself he'll be up soon and I'm not going anywhere, at least not today. I can't seem to help it, though. I want to take advantage of all the time we have together, especially since it's Christmas.

"What can I get you for breakfast?" Judy prompts.

I shake my head, not ready to eat anything yet. "I'm still full from last night," I admit. "I'm fine with coffee right now," I mumble. Then, I spin around and open the cabinet up above that holds all of the coffee cups. I reach for a red Christmas mug decorated with Christmas trees and pour myself a cup of coffee before turning back to them.

"Well, as soon as Max gets up, we can all exchange presents," Charles proposes, with a broad smile.

I shake my head and my heart sinks, as I suddenly feel vaguely out of place again. "Oh, I don't want to intrude. You can just let me know when you're done," I suggest, as I paste a smile on my face.

Judy arches her eyebrows and grins mischievously. She challenges, "Who says we don't have any presents for you?"

I gasp in surprise. "For me?" I pause. "Really?" I prod.

Judy laughs. "You can't wake up on Christmas morning and not have any presents," Judy claims, as if the idea were ridiculous.

My heart jumps up into my throat, making it hard to breathe. I'm overwhelmed with emotions from her statement. How did they have time to get me anything? They just met me and there's been a winter storm warning since even before I arrived. "Judy, I don't have anything for any of you," I murmur, regretfully.

"Don't be silly," Charles proclaims. He gives a slight wave of his hand, dismissing my claim as if it's no big deal.

"Ivy, you saved Christmas for this town by cooking. And then you cooked an amazing meal for our Christmas Eve dinner. Plus, all the other food you have made for us the last few days," she reiterates. "Believe me, all of those things were gifts enough," she insists.

I step up to Judy and give her a hug, attempting to fight back the tears trying to claw their way up my throat. "Thank you," I rasp, my voice cracking. I gulp down the lump in my throat and then try again. "Thank you so much," I whimper, appreciatively. I take a deep breath and exhale slowly, feeling a little better as I let her go.

"You're welcome," she replies. I take a step back and take another sip of my coffee. I set my coffee cup down, just as I hear ColeCole start to bark near the front of the house. My attention is immediately pulled in that direction, hoping it's Max just waking up.

I hear a door opening and then closing, coming from the front of the house. Then, I hear Max's deep voice calling out, "Mom! Dad? Is Ivy awake yet?" My heart skips a beat at the sound of his voice. He just got home. Where did he even go so early on Christmas morning? Is anything even open between the storm and the holiday?

"We're in the kitchen," she yells back.

Max enters carrying ColeCole. He leans against the counter near me. "Merry Christmas," he greets me, smiling down at me.

"Merry Christmas," I reply. I smile back at him, my heartbeat quickly accelerating.

"You were up and out early," Charles states, with a wry smile, piquing my curiosity.

"I had to pick some people up this morning. They didn't have a car," he informs us. He always seems to be towing cars or dropping off people who are having their cars fixed. I'm impressed he went out of his way to help someone on Christmas morning. I really read him wrong when I first met him. Every day he does so much to prove my first impression wrong and I absolutely love it.

"On Christmas?" Judy questions. "You're such a good boy, Max," she praises him, mirroring my own sentiment.

He smiles and gives his mom a hug. "Merry Christmas, Mom," he proclaims. He gives her a kiss on the top of her head, just before he releases her.

"Merry Christmas," she replies and smiles up at him.

"Merry Christmas, Dad," he adds.

His dad grins and murmurs, "Merry Christmas, Max."

"Can we open presents now?" Max requests. He claps his hands together in excitement, as his eyes alight with pure happiness.

I smile in amusement. He reminds me of a little kid on Christmas morning with how eager he seems to be.

"Sure," Judy responds, her own joy clear.

"I've got a surprise for Ivy," he announces, grinning down at me.

"For me?" I ask, shocked.

He nods, obviously happy with himself. He proposes, "I'd like to give my gift to Ivy first."

"To me?" I question. I feel a little silly with so much attention on me.

He nods his head in confirmation, appearing relaxed and truly happy. "Yeah," he mumbles, his voice catching. "You've treated me and my parents with such love and respect since you've been here and you didn't even know us," he emphasizes, with clear admiration in his voice.

I feel my face heat with embarrassment at his compliment. I shrug my shoulders, like it's no big deal. Anyone would do the same thing. "Max, it was the least I could do," I insist.

He grins and proclaims, "I'm really glad I met you, Ivy. You're a genuine person and I really want to get to know you more and have the chance to spend a lot more time with you," he confesses, causing my blush to deepen. "I hope this isn't the last holiday we spend together," he adds, with a playful smile.

My heartbeat quickens at his admission. I anxiously look down and then back up at him, fidgeting with my fingers, as I fill up more and more with hope with every word he utters. "Max," I gasp his name. "Stop," I appeal bashfully.

"No, let me finish," he requests. I snap my mouth shut and continue smiling at him. "When we first met, I honestly wasn't too nice. I was tired. I was hungry. I was cranky. I was cold. I was rude," he shakes his head in disbelief. "I could continue, but you already know all of that," he smirks, making me giggle. "I never would've seen you again if my mom didn't take you in and I was still rude," he emphasizes. "I'm really sorry for that," he apologizes emphatically, his regret obvious.

I shake my head, as I recall that night. "It's okay. Really," I declare. I smirk and remind him, "I was a little off that night too if I recall."

He chuckles and holds my gaze, "It's really not okay, but I'm grateful you gave me a chance anyway. You broke through at least one of the walls I've built up around my heart. You've shown me what I've been missing," he states. His admission causes a shiver to run down my spine and spread throughout my whole body.

"That was a real Christmas gift," he claims. "So, I wanted to get you something that I know you really want," he announces.

My eyebrows draw down in confusion, trying to come up with something I might have told him I wanted for Christmas, but I keep coming up blank. I shake my head and remind him, "I never told you what I wanted for Christmas."

His grin broadens, lighting up his eyes and letting it spread to the rest of his features. My breath catches in my throat. He takes a moment to stare into my eyes and I feel my face heat under his gaze. Then, with his smile bright, he proudly announces, "Oh, yes you did." He pauses and breaks his hold on me as he yells towards the front of the house, "Come on in!" Then, he turns and watches me in anticipation.

I glance towards the doorway, anxiously waiting for whoever might walk through the door. My mom rounds the corner and squeals with happiness the moment she sees me. I gasp in shock as tears instantly fill my eyes and overflow, cascading down my cheeks. My mom practically bounces towards me, followed by my dad and my twin brother, Sawyer. "Merry Christmas!" each of them joyously greets me, as they walk into the room.

"Sawyer! Mom! Daddy!" I cry out in both astonishment and glee. I rush to close the distance between us and throw my arms around each of them.

I hug my mom tightly, thrilled to see her! My tears continue to flow, completely unstoppable at this point. "Oh, my gosh! Honey, I missed you," she stammers, barely able to get the words out. Then, she releases me and I throw my arms around my dad.

He envelops me in his warm, protective hug. "I missed you so much," I cry.

"I was so worried about you," he claims, as he hugs me tightly. "So worried," he emphasizes.

He reluctantly releases me and I turn towards Sawyer and squeeze him with all my might. I'm barely able to see through the blur of my happy tears.

I release my brother and look at all of them to make sure this is real. I'm still in shock that they're all here. "I don't understand," I cry, looking back and forth between each of them and then back to Max. "How is this even possible?" I question, barely believing what I'm seeing.

My mom grins and nods towards Max. "Max here," she proudly announces, "called us last night after you went to bed. He got us a flight into Philadelphia first thing this morning," she apprises me.

I shake my head, still having trouble contemplating this perfect reality. "But Logan is closed," I state the obvious.

My dad nods in agreement. "Flights weren't coming in, Ivy. But they started going out again. Max found us one this morning," he reveals.

Sawyer gives a nod towards Max and jokes, "He's not such a bad guy after all." Max chuckles and I feel my face heat in embarrassment, remembering what I said when I first met him.

I shake my head in disbelief one more time with a smile plastered on my face, finally able to see through my tears. "I can't believe this," I murmur, taking in my family standing in front of me. I look over at Max and my heart skips a beat. I walk up to him and wrap my arms around his waist, hugging him gratefully and completely overwhelmed with emotion. I feel Max startle, before he relaxes into me and returns my hug. "Max, Thank you," I whisper into his chest. "Thank you so much," I repeat, for emphasis. I pull back slightly and grin up at him. "This was my Christmas wish," I enlighten him.

His grin turns mischievous and he confirms, "I know." He reaches into the pocket of his jeans and pulls out a folded slip of paper. It only takes a moment for me to realize exactly what it is.

"Max!" I scold. "You stole my wish!"

He chuckles, his smile becoming even brighter, causing my heart to jump into my throat. I attempt to gulp it down as I look up at him. Then he shakes his head gently and claims, "No, I granted it." I laugh in response and give him one more squeeze.

I startle and pull back, realizing I didn't even introduce my family. "Oh, Mom, Dad, Sawyer," I pause, "you already met Max," I begin. They all nod their heads in confirmation. I gesture towards Judy and Charles and finish the introductions. "This is Charles and Judy Carson. Charles and Judy, these are my parents, Mary and Bill Anderson and my twin brother, Sawyer."

"Thank you so much for taking such good care of our little girl," my dad emphatically thanks them, as he shakes both of their hands.

Max's arm remains around me. I lean back into his embrace, with goosebumps prickling my skin, underneath my warm pajamas. I watch my mom in her gray jeans and white, light blue and gray striped sweater talking to Judy in her Christmas pajamas. Then, I look over at my dad in his rust colored Henley and jeans and Sawyer in a dark green thermal and jeans, both talking with Charles in his matching Christmas PJ's. The scene around me makes me laugh and completely warms me to my soul. I'm not able to wipe the smile off my face, but I don't want to. I'm absolutely thrilled for this unexpected surprise.

I look up at Max in awe. I'm so amazed by him. He grins and prompts, "What?"

I shake my head in disbelief, feeling overwhelmed with his gesture. "I can't believe you did this for me," I admit.

"Believe it, Princess," he proclaims. He grins, with a confidence that warms me inside and out. This is a Christmas I will never forget.

Chapter 24

Ivy

After we help to clean up the dinner dishes and make room for dessert at the table, I return to my chair at the dining room table. Tonight, Judy decorated the large table with a Christmas red tablecloth and a beautiful ivory lacy tablecloth overlay, so the red peeks through, matching the bows on the chandelier and the bows on the garland around the windows. The long candelabrum rests in the middle of the table, with the candlelight of all five candles flickering low. The whole room looks not only festive, but also absolutely stunning by any standards.

I love how everyone dressed up for Christmas dinner, following Judy's long-time family tradition. I understand the tradition a little more now, just by being a part of it. It feels like dressing up enhances how special Christmas truly is, just by doing something simple. Judy sits on one end of the table in silky black dress pants and a Christmas red button down silk blouse, matching much of the room. Charles sits on the opposite end of the table, facing his wife in tan dress pants, a red and navy plaid dress shirt, covered up with a gray sweater stitched with diamond shapes and a button at the top near his neck. My mom is sitting next to Charles on his left, wearing black dress pants and a Christmas green, V-neck, button down cashmere sweater with ruffles along the edges. My dad sits to her left and to Judy's right, wearing tan pants, a light blue button down shirt and a navy, V-neck, red and white striped sweater vest. I grin thinking about how much it reminds me of something he wears to work every day. On the opposite side of the table from my parents,

I'm sitting between my brother and Max. Sawyer looks classy dressed in charcoal dress pants and a burgundy, ribbed sweater with a zipper at his neck. While Max looks handsome as always in dark jeans and a dark green sweater, causing the color of his eyes to pop even more. I have on a simple, but elegant blush pantsuit with an ivory, cashmere sweater over top and tan patterned heels. I decided to leave my blonde hair down today and I added some curls to give it the appearance of being more full.

As Max's mom and dad slip away to bring in the dessert, Max leans close to me. He whispers in my ear, "You look really beautiful, Ivy."

My cheeks instantly heat with his compliment, as I feel butterflies take over my insides. I smile at him and whisper appreciatively, "Thank you, Max."

Judy and Charles walk back into the room carrying fancy Christmas dishes, filled with various desserts. My eyes go wide as I take in the pumpkin pie, chocolate cake and colorful Christmas cookies. I almost forgot we hid some of those, so we would have enough for today. My mouth waters as I inhale the sweet scents of cinnamon, gingerbread, pumpkin and chocolate. Judy strides back into the kitchen and returns almost immediately carrying a pot of coffee in an ivory pot that matches the china. "Everyone ready for dessert?" Charles prompts, cheerfully, after Judy returns to her seat.

"Yes, please," Max and Sawyer state in unison. They're both practically drooling, causing all of us to laugh. They both shrug innocently in response and begin passing around the desserts. I place a small piece of chocolate cake on my plate and inhale deeply, enjoying the delectable scents. Everyone immediately digs in, myself included.

"Judy, everything was absolutely delicious tonight," I murmur, gratefully. It always feels a little strange not to be the one doing the cooking, but I also know how much work she put into making everything. I feel like knowing what I do about putting a meal like this together, only helps me appreciate the food even more.

She smiles appreciatively at me, as she pours herself a cup of coffee. Then she offers it to my dad, sitting to her right. "Well, thank you, Ivy. I'm glad I could make dinner for you for once, after all that wonderful food you have made for us the last few days," she expresses, sincerely.

I blush and take another bite of the chocolate cake in front of me, trying to accept her compliment. I would've helped with dinner if she would've let me, but she insisted I spend the time with my family and Max. It also gave Max some time to get to know my family better. I love how much he hit it off with Sawyer, too. I don't know if he realizes how much that means to me, but it really does mean more than I'm able to express.

"This certainly was a memorable Christmas," my mom announces, as she sets her fork down on her plate.

I huff a laugh and instantly agree, "That's for sure." My mind wanders to the unexpectedness of the last few days. It's crazy to think about how different the last few days might've been if it weren't for the snowstorm, especially how different Christmas would've been for all of us.

"Let's do it again next year, but at our house," my dad proposes. Then, he takes a bite of his pumpkin pie and savors the flavor.

My heart skips a beat and I can't help, but grin at the possibility of spending another holiday with Max. "Oh, that sounds fun," Judy happily agrees.

"As long as there isn't any snow!" Sawyer interjects. We all burst out laughing in response, before nodding in agreement.

"And Ivy does the cooking!" Max suggests. Then, he turns and grins at me, before he gives me a playful wink. I blush a deeper shade of red as everyone laughs. Max shrugs his shoulders, "What?" he asks, innocently. "I really like her cooking," he emphasizes.

Charles chuckles softly and nods in agreement. "I'm pretty sure we all do," he adds.

"Thank you," I murmur, politely accepting their compliment.

Judy sets her fork down on her plate and leans forward. Then, she takes a deep breath and focuses her attention on me. "So, Ivy, Charles and I were talking after you went to bed last night and we have a proposal for you," she enlightens me.

"Oh?" I question, full of curiosity.

Charles nods in confirmation, "We do."

"Okay..." I mumble, slowly, dragging out the word. I have no idea what kind of proposal they could have for me. My heartbeat speeds up nervously in anticipation.

"Being the mayor of this town, I don't have the chance to follow some of my own dreams," she states, matter of fact. My heart aches knowing what she gave up to become the mayor, but I believe she wouldn't want me to feel bad. It was her choice, but that doesn't always mean it was easy. I nod in understanding, hoping to convey for her to continue. "When I accepted the office, I knew that I was in it for the long haul. My dream of opening my own restaurant was going to have to be put on hold for a long time and I was good with that," she concedes. She offers Charles a small smile for emphasis.

I glance anxiously over at Max, who's unsuccessfully attempting to hide his growing smile. His actions only succeed in making me more nervous. He obviously knows what they're talking about. Then, I look back at Judy and prompt her to keep going, anxious to know what's going on. "Okay..." I murmur slowly, dragging out the word again.

"I saved up a lot of money to open my own restaurant and since I went in a different direction, I never spent it. I invested the money and made it work for me," she informs me. "Now, I want to invest in you," she broadcasts. She gives me a look full of pride, as if she were my own mother.

"What does that mean?" I inquire, still completely confused.

"I would like to open a restaurant with you, here in Bethlehem. I'll be your investor and you create the restaurant," she announces, her eyes lighting up with excitement. I gasp and my mouth instantly drops open in astonishment. "Max will handle the business end of it all," she continues, casually.

I focus on my breathing, her announcement completely overwhelming me. She wants to invest in a restaurant with me? "Wh...what?" I stammer, my eyes going as wide as saucers. I take a deep breath, attempting to calm my racing heart at the thought of working with Max and being able to do what I love. This is literally a dream come true! This just doesn't seem real.

"No way!" Sawyer blurts out, sounding just as shocked as I feel.

"What an amazing opportunity!" my mom exclaims.

I take one look at Max and my heart pounds even harder, even becoming erratic, as so many possibilities flash through my mind. "Did you know about this?" I question him, believing I already know the answer.

He grins and nods his head in confirmation. He shrugs and admits, "That's what I was looking up last night on the computer. There's a restaurant for sale in town, right on Main Street," he enlightens me, causing me to gasp for breath.

"You said you wanted to leave Charleston," Judy reminds me. I bite my lip and glance over at Max hesitantly. Does he want me to stay? Is he falling for me, like I'm falling for him or is this just business? He's watching me with a hopeful smile on his face and a question in his eyes, making my heart beat even faster.

"You've told us that plenty of times, Ivy," my dad reiterates.

I force a nervous smile and concede, "I know." I take a deep breath and exhale slowly trying to process their proposal. This is what I've always wanted, but there's so much to think about. What will it look like? Will I have a theme? What kind of menu do I want to have? What about permits and prices and everything else I have no clue about? Does Max really want to help me? Does he want to work with me? My heart races in anticipation. Can I really do this? I take a deep breath and quietly admit, "This is going to be awfully hard." It's honestly a little overwhelming.

"If it wasn't hard, it wouldn't be worth it," both my mom and Judy declare in unison. I've heard those same words of encouragement so many times from my mom. They both look at each other with wide eyes, before they burst out laughing.

I smirk and glance quickly around the table. "I told you that you were alike!" I exclaim. Everyone laughs in response, helping me feel a little bit lighter.

We catch our breaths and Sawyer focuses intently on me. "Ivy, this is a dream come true for you. You have to take the chance," he encourages me.

216

"And it's so much closer than Charleston," my mom reminds me of the obvious, happily sharing her opinion. I agree. I would love to be closer to home. That was the hardest part of living in Charleston for me. I missed my family so much, especially around the holidays.

"We'll help you however we can," Charles offers, supportively.

"So will we," my dad declares. I glance up at him. His shoulders are pushed back and he's beaming at me, full of pride, spreading warmth throughout my body.

"And I will invest under one condition," Judy adds. She pauses and waits until she has my full attention.

"What's that?" I prompt, curiously.

"That you let me come help you cook and even work on the menu with you," she announces her simple expectations.

I grin, easily coming to a decision. I nod my head firmly in agreement, knowing this is an opportunity I could never let pass me by. "Oh my, gosh," I mumble, trying to believe this is actually happening. "Yes! Yes," I finally confirm, eagerly. "Let's do it!" I jump out of my seat and step around Max's chair to reach Judy. I wrap my arms tightly around her in an appreciative hug.

I can't believe my dreams are coming true. It feels like I've waited so long and now everything seems to be occurring all at once. "This is happening so fast. I'll have to find a place to live and work in the meantime," I begin rambling, excitedly. I release Judy and practically bounce back to my seat. I glance around the table at everyone, my heart feeling more full as my eyes land on each person sitting around the table. Every one of them means so much to me. That's crazy to think, when I didn't even know half of them a few days ago.

"I'm sure it will all work out," Charles reassures me as I meet his eyes. "Don't worry," he maintains. "We're not going anywhere," he emphasizes, letting me know I have a place to stay for as long as I need.

My eyes land on Max last. My cheeks are beginning to hurt, but I couldn't wipe the smile off my face if I had to. I feel his fingers grasp mine under the table. I bite my lower lip to hold back my outward reaction. He looks into my eyes and gives my hand an encouraging squeeze. "You can say that again," Max whispers, with completely different intentions. My heart skips a beat and begins pounding in my ears, as I stare into his eyes. I feel my whole body warm locked in his gaze.

Out of the corner of my eye, I notice my dad lift his wine glass and hold it up for a toast. I reluctantly tear my gaze away from Max and focus on my dad, just as he proposes a toast to all of us. "Merry Christmas, everyone!" he proclaims, smiling fondly over at me.

I easily return his smile, as we all reach for our wine glasses and repeat his toast. "Merry Christmas!" we cheer in unison. We gently clink glasses across the middle of the table. Then, I bring my glass to my lips and take a small sip, enjoying the fruity undertones.

After seeing my family walk into the kitchen this morning, I didn't think this Christmas could get any better, but clearly I was more than wrong. My heart stutters, feeling full of love and happiness. I take another small sip of my wine before setting my glass down on the table. I sit back and look around the table, attempting to just enjoy listening to Max's family talking and laughing with my own. I'm incredibly grateful to have everyone here in my life. A few days ago, I never would've thought that I would be more than thankful for the winter storm of the century. I guess I found my reason for it all.

Hopefully, it's more than one reason, I can't help but think, with another glance at Max.

Chapter 25

Ivy

I slip away from everyone to take a few much-needed quiet minutes to myself. The whole day has been perfect. I couldn't have dreamed of a Christmas this wonderful, but it's also a little overwhelming. I lean against the windowsill and stare out the front windows in the sitting room. It's no longer snowing, but the snow is piled high on every surface. It's heavily weighing down many trees and bushes, even bringing many branches close to the ground. The moonlight glistens off the snow, creating a beautiful Christmas glow, giving the streets a magical look. I have to admit, today does feel a little bit like a dream to me, but I don't think anyone could blame me after everything that's happened. I'm trying to take a little time to process everything that has transpired today. I think I really need it.

I still can't believe Max flew my whole family here to surprise me for Christmas. When I think about the night I met him, I would've never believed this is where we'd be only a few days later. He's so much more than I could have ever imagined. He said he wanted me to have something to open on Christmas, but I don't believe he just did it for that reason alone. It feels like more. When he held my wish out to me, with that contagious smile lighting up his face, I just knew he did it for me. He did it to make my wish come true because he cares about me. I just know it. No one has ever done something so incredible for me before, but Max did. It feels like my heart swells, filling up with love every time I think about him. I giggle to myself, again thinking how wrong I was about him. The overwhelming part of the last few days is the realization that seeing him walking in with my family this morning, was only the beginning for us. It's almost as if I'm really falling for him. I gasp and my heart begins to pound rapidly, as I recognize that's the truth.

I gulp hard and take a deep, steadying breath. I give myself a light shake and attempt to veer my thoughts in a new direction. If I keep thinking about Max, I'll start questioning how he feels and what he's thinking. He still hasn't kissed me. Well, not when we were both ready, anyway. What if he just wants me as a business partner now? Everything seems to be falling perfectly into place with Max, and moving closer to my family, as well as Judy and Charles investing in Max and me. I don't want to ruin anything if he doesn't feel the same way I do, but I sure hope he does. I don't know if I've ever wanted anything to be more real, than his feelings for me.

I force myself to stop thinking about my feelings for Max and instead focus on the other huge change in my life as of today. I put all my attention in the restaurant we're going to open together. I have so many different ideas running rampant in my head, at just the thought of owning my own restaurant. I have always wanted this, but now that it seems like my dreams are about to become my reality, my brain has gone into overdrive contemplating the scope of it. I keep trying to narrow everything down and come up with what I'd really like to create with this restaurant. What kind of food, what kind of décor and what kind of atmosphere? What will we name it and what will the menu look like? Who will our customers be and will the staff become like a second family to us? What will our theme be and will we be able to carry it through to every part of the restaurant? Will we be able to cater parties and eventually big events?

Will Max and I work well together and will we be able to make our restaurant a success?

I sigh and give myself another shake to stop my incessant ramblings. I'm extremely grateful Judy and Charles want to invest in my cooking and in me. That takes a lot of confidence and trust in me. Although we've only known each other for a few days, it feels like it has been so much longer. I huff a laugh. I guess staying at their house unexpectedly for a few days, during Christmas because of this snowstorm has really brought us all closer together. Of course, technically, Judy and Charles are not just investing in me. They're also investing in Max. He'll be the one to handle everything outside the kitchen, such as permits, paperwork, orders, scheduling, accounting, marketing, and probably so much more I don't understand. I know they have one hundred percent confidence in him, just like I do. I honestly have been wondering how I ever doubted him at all.

I'm looking forward to talking to Max, and Judy about all my ideas, but I want to have something prepared when I sit down with them, so I sound like I know what I'm talking about. Plus, I should probably have a few different ideas, so we can find one that will mesh with all of us. I shake my head, still a little bit in shock that Judy and Charles want to put so much into me, even with Max as my partner. I am really looking forward to working with Judy in the kitchen too. I want to try a few different recipes with her and figure out what complements each food. I'm sure we'll be able to come up with an amazing menu in no time.

I can't believe Max knew about all of this and he didn't tell me anything. It amazes me that he was the one who put the idea in his parents' heads. He was even the one who did the research and found the perfect place for the restaurant. My stomach flip-flops anxiously, wondering what it will be like inside. Of course we can make whatever changes we want, but I'm still excited to see it. Max left a message for the realtor to request an appointment for us to go look at it. Now, we just have to wait patiently for them to get back to us, but I'm so excited! I'm really struggling to sit still. I'm sure we won't hear from anyone until morning since it is Christmas.

I think Max and I will work really well together. I'm actually kind of in awe of him when I think about everything he's done. I'm grateful he seems to be just as excited, as I am to work together on this project. I wouldn't be able to do this without him. He knows how to do all the things I have no clue about. In fact, it sounds like he's incredible at running a business. I have to admit I'm thrilled we'll be able to spend a lot of time together. I guess this means we'll be partners. I bite my lip in anticipation. I hope he really does want this as much as I do. I huff a laugh as I realize, every thought I have, seems to keep circling back to him.

I sigh happily and push away from the window. I'm suddenly extremely anxious to see Max again, even if it hasn't been very long. I walk around the stairs and turn the corner towards the family room. I stop and smirk at the sight of Max in front of me. He's leaning against the half wall on his forearms, right under the mistletoe. How does he always end up there? Does he do it on purpose? I giggle to myself. Then, I force myself to move my feet and approach him, my heart immediately starts thudding loudly against my ribcage. I lean up against the half-wall right next to him, propping my elbows on the wall in front of me.

He doesn't even glance in my direction and I realize he's either staring at something or he's really deep in thought. I bump him lightly in the shoulder with mine, attempting to get his attention. He finally glances down at me and offers me a small smile. Then, he looks back in the same direction. I follow his gaze and notice he's watching our families. They're all standing by the brightly lit Christmas tree, with the dancing yellow, orange and even some blue flames of a fire, crackling in the fireplace behind them. They're talking and laughing with one another, like close friends. The sight warming me from the inside, out and I can't help but smile.

"Hey," I mumble to Max.

The corners of his mouth twitch up in amusement at my casual greeting. He doesn't even look at me as he replies, "Hey."

I watch our families in silence along with him for a few more moments. I'm not able to hear what they're saying, but I can't help but enjoy all their joyful expressions, as they talk animatedly with one another. "Isn't it funny how well our families get along?" I prompt, thoughtfully.

He chuckles lightly and agrees with a slight nod of his head. "It's like they've known each other for years," he acknowledges.

I giggle as he voices the same words I was just thinking. I nod in agreement and murmur, "I know. It's so strange."

"It is," he agrees, nodding his head. He glances at me out of the corner of his eye and I see a quick flash of hesitation before it's gone. Then, he glances back towards them, before he quietly professes, "It's how I feel about you, too."

I audibly gasp at his confession, while butterflies instantly take over my insides. What does that even mean? I attempt to gulp down the lump in my throat, before I try to clarify his statement. "Like you've known me forever?" I question, my voice barely audible. My

224

heart skips a beat and I bite my bottom lip nervously, anxiously waiting for his response.

He turns fully towards me and meets my eyes. I release my lip and wait for him to answer my question, feeling hopeful. "Yeah," he confirms, confidently.

My whole body warms and my heart quickens, as my feelings seem to grow even more with his admission. He stares at me, assessing me as he waits for my reaction. I think I'm falling in love with him. I bite my lower lip again, fighting my smile. I suddenly freeze, as my mind drifts back again, to what Judy said to me the other day. My breath hitches at the memory. "I think that maybe your mom is right," I rasp, "and you are the reason," I admit, taking my chance. The restaurant isn't the reason, he is.

He tilts his head to the side, as his eyebrows draw down in confusion, a small smile still playing on his lips. "What do you mean?" he prods.

"Maybe we were supposed to meet, Max," I claim, holding his gaze. Do I really think this whole snowstorm happened just to bring me here to meet Max and get to know him better? I huff a laugh and give myself a light shake. Maybe I do. Then, I shrug and mumble, "I don't know." I take a deep breath, trying to put the words together to explain to him what I'm thinking and how I'm really feeling. "It just feels," I pause, thoughtfully. Then, I turn completely towards him. I look him in the eyes and square my shoulders, doing everything I can to convey the truth of how I really feel to him. I finally open myself up to him and confess with complete confidence, "It feels right."

Max's lips twitch up, while his eyes remain focused on me. My breathing becomes ragged as he slowly closes the distance between us. My heart pounds so hard, I can hear the flow of my blood in my ears. It feels as if my heart might burst right out of my chest, just to get closer to him. Then, we finally meet. I gasp softly at the gentle brush of his lips against mine. His hands slide up my arms until he tenderly cradles my face in his hands, warming me with his simple touch. He moves his mouth in a slow rhythm over mine, while I meet him every step of the way. He pulls his head back slightly, breaking our connection and giving us both a chance to catch our breath.

His green eyes sparkle joyfully down on me. I smile up at him, this intense feeling of happiness overpowering me and bringing my whole body to life, inside and out. I love it. His hands fall to my waist and mine drops between us, to his chest. "Yes," he agrees. "It does feel right," he whispers.

I blush, thinking about everything he's done for me. He's made this Christmas more than special. He brought our families together by finding a way to bring mine here. He discovered a place for my dreams and his to come true and for us to make them happen side by side. My heart jumps up into my throat and I struggle to gulp it down, grateful for so much. I feel truly blessed this Christmas. "Thank you for making my Christmas wish come true," I repeat. It feels as if I will never be able to thank him enough.

"You're welcome," he smiles, causing my heart to skip a beat. Then, he tilts his head to the side, as a mischievous glint sparks in his eyes. "Thank you for making my Christmas wish come true, too," he murmurs, appreciatively.

My eyebrows draw down in confusion. I don't even know what he wished for. How would I make it come true? I quickly elaborate. "I'm talking about the one that I wrote on the paper last night," I explain.

His grin broadens and he fights to hold back his laughter. Then, he nods his head and playfully confirms, "So am I."

I watch as he reaches into his pocket and pulls out a piece of paper that appears to be another one of the wishes. He carefully unfolds the paper and holds it out for me to read. I grasp one side of the paper, while he holds the other. I glance up at him in anticipation, before I focus on what he wrote. My breath hitches as I process the words. I read, "A kiss from Ivy under the mistletoe."

My stomach does a somersault as awareness washes over me. I look up at him in wide-eyed surprise. "Oh!" I exclaim. Goosebumps spread over my whole body. I can't believe he wrote this last night. I give a slight shake of my head in disbelief. Then, I suddenly can't stop myself from giggling at the craziness of it all. Max joins in, chuckling along with me.

When we both stop laughing, he stares at me adoringly, causing my heart to clench with pure joy. "Merry Christmas, Ivy," he repeats the sentiment.

"Merry Christmas," I echo, feeling breathless. I look up at him, smiling, as I attempt to open myself up and show him how much he already means to me. Then, he tips his head down towards me and I push up on my toes to close the distance between us. Our lips meet, warming me from my head to my toes as we kiss again, under the mistletoe.

Who would've thought that getting stranded on the side of the road in the middle of a snowstorm, and then being stuck in Bethlehem, Pennsylvania and not being able to make it home for Christmas, would turn out to be the best things that ever happened to me? Not me, but the truth is I'm looking forward to my future with Max. It turns out all I needed was a lot of snow, a handsome man named Max who loves to challenge me and a little bit of mistletoe to find everything I've ever dreamed of.

The End

Acknowledgements

I would like to take this opportunity to thank everyone who has helped with this book. First, I would like to thank Kenney Myers for investing in this Christmas movie. Without you, the movie or the book would never have come to be. Thank you to Amy Minter, Producer of the film. I greatly appreciate all of your support! Thank you to my good friend, Candy Cain (Yes, that's really her name). She came to me with a budget in mind and asked me to collaborate with her on a Christmas movie/book project. The idea started with the two of us at breakfast, a pen, and a notebook. By the end of breakfast, we had our outline. It wasn't long before she wrote and directed the movie and then I wrote this book. Thank you for asking me to be a part of this wonderful adventure and for being such a magnificent friend.

I would like to thank Cody Calafiore and Julianne Michelle who helped bring Max and Ivy to life in the film and on the pages. I really enjoyed working with everyone in the cast and crew of the film and I thank each and every one of you. I loved seeing the movie for the first time on the big screen. I'm so used to telling stories with words, instead of pictures, but it was incredibly exciting seeing the story in a different way throughout this process. Thank you to the Rund family who were all incredibly gracious throughout filming in their beautiful home. Your home made it easy to draw inspiration for the setting.

Thank you to Lauren Halla Celi, owner and photographer of "A Moment in Time Photography". You did a beautiful job on the cover photo. Thank you to Constantine Chutis for the incredible job on the Graphic Design for both the paperback and digital book cover.

As always, thank you to Nancy Vincent and all my Beta Readers. I greatly appreciate all of your input and reviews. I value each and every one of you.

Thank you, most of all, to my friends and family for their continuous support. I wouldn't be here without ALL of you. I love you all! Plus, an extra thank you to my family who has stepped up with me working on set and being away from home more often.

I hope everyone enjoys reading and watching Ivy & Mistletoe. And, no matter what time of year it is when you read this, Merry Christmas!

Connect with the Author

For more family contemporary romance, read more by Nicole Mullaney and Ethan Dulane. Connect with Nicole here:

Follow Me on Instagram
@nicolemullaney

For more adult contemporary romance, read books by Nikki A Lamers. Connect with Nikki here:

Official Author Website
www.nikkialamersauthor.com

Author Facebook Page
www.facebook.com/pg/NikkiALamersAuthor

Follow Me on Instagram
@NikkialamersAuthor

Author Goodreads Page
www.goodreads.com/author/show/8451774.Nikki_A_La mers

Amazon Author Page
https://www.amazon.com/Nikki-A.-Lamers/e/B00NU1VU8M

For more information on Gemelli Films, find them here:

Official Website
http://Gemellifilm.com/

Gemelli Films Facebook Page
https://m.facebook.com/GemelliFilms/

Follow #gemellifilms on Instagram